LONG TRAIL TO REDEMPTION

A U.S. senator and his family have been kidnapped by bandits and imprisoned in the Mexican village of Las Palomas, but the government is reluctant to provoke war by sending troops after them. Joshua Bell of the secret service amasses a team to retrieve the captives: assassin-for-hire Hawk; bounty hunter Wolf McGee; town-tamer Utah Smith; former shootist Walter Cronkite; secret service agent Jess Stuart; and drifter gunfighter Red Kinane. But not all of them can be trusted . . .

B. S. DUNN

LONG TRAIL TO REDEMPTION

Complete and Unabridged

LINFORD
Leicester

First published in Great Britain in 2015

First Linford Edition
published 2018

A catalogue record for this book is available
from the British Library.

ISBN 978–1–4448–3790–2

Published by
F. A. Thorpe (Publishing)
Anstey, Leicestershire

Set by Words & Graphics Ltd.
Anstey, Leicestershire
Printed and bound in Great Britain by
T. J. International Ltd., Padstow, Cornwall

This book is printed on acid-free paper

This one is for Sam and Jacob.

1

'Damn it, you murderin' son of a bitch, get your yellow carcass out here now!'

The challenge carried from the deserted street, across the bat-wings and into the Silver Bullet Saloon. All eyes focused on the man who stood at the hardwood bar with his back to the main entrance. To many he looked like an ordinary drifter; a saddle-bum, some might describe him. Battered sweat-stained brown Stetson, unshaven face, red hair, worn clothes, average height and build.

The tied-down Colt .45 told a different story. His name was Red Kinane and he was a gunfighter.

He'd ridden into Silver Creek three days earlier on a trail-weary Mustang, at the bequest of a woman whose husband had been murdered in cold blood by the son of a rich landowner who wanted their range for himself.

Kinane had met Angie Sweeney when she paid him his money. The gunfighter had no qualms about killing the young man; by what he'd learned, the young punk had it coming.

Word quickly raced around town that the red-headed stranger was asking questions about the young man called Keno. The barkeep, wiping down the polished hardwood bar top with a stained black-and-white rag, stopped near Kinane and spoke softly. 'I guess 'young Keno' means you.'

Kinane sat his half-empty beer glass on the bar and wiped the froth from his top lip with the back of his hand.

'Are you goin' out there?' the barkeep asked with a hint of eagerness.

Kinane looked at the old man with ice-blue eyes, windows into his soul. 'Sure; what's one more ghost to haunt me?'

'Why do you do it then?' asked a confused barkeep. 'Why don't you stop?'

Kinane's answer only made for more

questions. 'Because they won't let me.'

'What do you mean, they won't let you?'

There was no answer as Kinane had turned away and headed for the doors. He stepped out onto the boardwalk and stopped. He looked left and right.

Keno was thirty yards away, standing in the middle of Silver Creek's main street.

'About time you showed, old man.'

Keno was young, not much more than a kid really, but he was playing a man's game.

Kinane reached into the left pocket of his trail-stained coat and lightly touched the chain and crucifix that he kept there.

'Well, what are you waitin' for? I'm right here, ain't I?'

Kinane moved down from the board-walk and out into the dust of Main Street. He turned and walked toward Keno and adjusted his coat clear of the Colt. A practiced eye took in the sur-roundings while remaining focused on the kid.

At thirty yards Keno said, 'That's far enough. Don't bother comin' closer. I can kill you real good just there.'

Kinane didn't break stride. He kept an even pace, his feet kicking up small puffs of dust with each step. At fifteen yards, Keno was nervous. 'I said, that's far enough. Don't you hear too good?'

Kinane kept walking.

Keno licked his lips nervously. His mouth was dry. At thirteen yards, Keno's voice rose sharply in pitch. 'I said stop, damnit.'

Kinane kept walking. At ten yards, Keno let out a screech, 'Damn you, stop!'

He went for his gun. And was fast — but compared to Kinane, Keno's fast was far too slow.

Kinane's Colt came up and erupted. The slug hit Keno in the chest and shattered his breastbone before his gun could come level. Keno rose to his toes, staggered back a few steps, then fell into the dust.

Thirty minutes later, as Kinane was about to ride out of town on his horse, the telegrapher found him at the livery.

'There you are, Mister Kinane. I was hoping you hadn't left yet.'

'Why's that?'

'I have a telegram for you.'

He handed over the piece of paper and left.

Kinane looked at the telegram.

JOB FOR YOU STOP GO TO GOLD CREEK NEW MEXICO STOP WORTH FIVE THOUSAND DOLLARS STOP JOSHUA BELL UNITED STATES SECRET SERVICE

Kinane folded the paper and put it in his pocket. The Arizona job would have to wait.

* * *

Hawk woke to the sound of keys in the lock of the cold grey steel door. He swung his legs over the side of the bunk and sat on the edge. Two guards entered the small stone-block prison cell, one carrying leg irons.

He tossed them onto the floor. 'Here, put them on. Warden wants to see you.'

Hawk never moved. 'What's he want with me?'

'How the hell should we know? Just put the irons on,' answered the other guard.

Hawk regarded the guard coldly. He'd spent the last two years in prison, and they'd been two lousy, miserable, gut-eating years.

'Move, Prisoner 84265.'

'I have a name,' Hawk said caustically.

'No, you don't. You have a number and that is all.'

Damn the both of you, Hawk thought, wishing he had his brace of .45s. He wanted to shoot the pair of them where they stood. Hawk was a cold-blooded killer, a gunman who'd made a name for himself from Kansas to Mexico. He took on any job offered, provided the money was right.

In the past, he'd dressed mainly in black, and worn a silver-studded double gun-rig containing a pair of Colts, the grips inlaid with the image of a hawk. Now he was dressed in prison rags, his face unshaven, and his brown hair was a straggly mess. His cold blue eyes still glittered and his well-built frame was slimmed down some. He was a far cry from the man who had been sentenced to fifteen years for accidentally killing a sheriff's deputy.

Hawk put the leg irons on and stood in the center of the small cell.

'Alright,' said a guard. 'You know where to go. You've been there enough. Move out.'

Hawk walked slowly from the cell, his every step accompanied by the jangle of the steel chains.

* * *

'Unchain him and leave.'

The two guards shot the warden an alarmed look.

The warden, a solid, middle-aged man, nodded his consent. 'You heard the man; do it and wait outside.'

The two guards unchained Hawk's legs and walked back out of the warden's office.

'Sit down, Mister Hawk.' It was the stranger who spoke again; the one who'd ordered them to unchain him.

'Why?' Hawk asked insolently.

'Damnit man,' the warden snapped, 'don't ask why, just do it. Or I'll call Holt and Wilbur back in here, and they will sit your ass down.'

Taking his time, Hawk finally sat on the hard wooden chair.

'My name,' began the stranger, 'is Joshua Bell.'

Hawk stared at Bell, yet to be impressed. The man was dressed in a suit that hung perfectly on his bulky frame. His black hair was combed neatly and he was clean-shaven. What Hawk noticed most was the bulge of the pistol under his coat.

'So?' said Hawk, showing total disrespect.

'By hell, Hawk, I'll . . . '

Bell held up a hand to stop the warden from continuing his rant. 'Thank you, Warden Stubbs. I can take it from here.'

He looked hard at Hawk, his eyes unblinking. 'Mister Hawk, I have a proposition for you. Are you interested or not?'

'What could you do for me? I'm here for fifteen years for killin' a deputy sheriff.'

'I know, Mister Hawk. Are you interested or not?'

'Sure, why not?' Hawk answered, not really caring.

'Mister Hawk, I work for the United States Government. I can get you out of here right now, and get you a full pardon and a chance to earn five thousand dollars.'

Hawk sat up straight. His interest was sufficiently piqued. 'How?'

'The government has a small job that needs doing. You, if you accept, will be part of a small group recruited for that purpose.'

Hawk raised his eyebrows. 'That's it

— just do a small job, and I walk free?'

Bell nodded. 'That's it.'

Now Hawk was skeptical. 'What's the catch?'

'No catch, Mister Hawk, just the real possibility you could all die before it's over.'

Bell let it sink in for a moment. 'Well, what do you say?'

Hawk smiled a cunning, thoughtful smile. 'Sure why not?'

'One more thing, Mister Hawk. If you see this as a chance to escape, think again. If you run, you will be hunted down and killed like the animal that you are.'

Hawk kept smiling.

'Do we understand each other Mister Hawk?'

Hawk kept smiling.

Bell took a folded piece of paper from his pocket and passed it to Hawk. 'You will meet me there in ten days. If you take eleven, we will not be there, so make sure you are, Mister Hawk. Make sure that you are.'

2

Lone Springs was a one-horse town in the middle of nowhere. An ideal spot for the McClane Brothers to hole up in. The entire place consisted of a main street, one saloon, a small livery, a hotel, a general store, and no law.

Wolf McGee knew without a shadow of a doubt exactly where the McClanes would be. Drinking and whoring, spending the money they'd taken from the Western Stage four days before.

McGee headed straight for the saloon. He wondered to himself whether they would go quietly or kicking. Not that it mattered. Dead was easier.

Every person in the stinking, run-down saloon turned to watch as he eased his way through the front entry, holding a sawed-off shotgun.

The sight they saw was an unshaven man of average height and build, dressed in beat-up clothes. His dark eyes were hidden in shadow beneath the brim of his sweat-stained hat.

McGee slowly scanned the small bar room, searching for his quarry.

There were four men sitting at a table playing poker, one with a whore draped over his shoulder. Two other men sat at a table in a far corner, sharing a watered-down bottle of rye. Another two stood at a rough-hewn bar, talking to an old barkeep.

One by one they returned to their own business, not bothered by the trail-hardened bounty hunter who'd walked in.

McGee lowered the shotgun and strode up to the bar.

The barkeep turned his attention away from the two men he was talking to and approached McGee. The old man had sad, watery eyes and thinning grey hair with moustache to match. 'What can I get you, stranger?'

McGee tossed a twenty-dollar piece upon the scratched bar top. 'A bottle and some information.'

The old man hesitated. 'The bottle I can do; the information, I'm not so sure about.'

'I'm lookin' for two men, strangers.'

Nervously, the two men closest eased slowly along the bar.

'Look around you, mister, everyone in here is a stranger.'

'The fellers I'm lookin' for are brothers, go by the name of McClane. One brother has red hair, the other yeller. Both will be splashin' money around.'

The barkeep uncorked a pale watered-down bottle of rye and poured a finger's worth into a shot glass. He picked up the cork, studied it for a moment, and said, 'I got two rooms out the back. The fellers you're lookin' for are in them with two of my girls. Have been since they rode in last night.'

McGee nodded and threw back the shot; which, although watered down, still burned.

'Mister,' the barkeep continued, 'you be careful of those girls. Whatever happens, remember they ain't got nothin' to do with it.'

McGee ignored him. 'Through that door?' he enquired, indicating the far end of the bar.

The barkeep nodded. 'Yep, that's it.'

McGee cocked the hammers of his shotgun and walked towards the door.

'You mind what I said, mister. You be careful of those girls,' the barkeep called to his back.

'You just stay out of my way,' was all Wolf McGee said.

He quietly turned the handle and gently pushed the door open. Rusty hinges creaked in protest. On the other side of the door was a short, dimly lit passage, with a door at the end and one on each side.

Wolf McGee moved silently as he walked through the opening. He paused outside the first door and heard muffled voices. Then one of the girls giggled with delight.

McGee moved on. He paused outside the second door; again, muffled voices.

He came to the third door and tried the knob. It turned easily. Opening the door, McGee saw that it led outside to an outhouse in a sad state of disrepair. McGee closed it softly, turned to face the way he'd come, and levelled the already cocked shotgun.

'Chance and Delbert McClane, put your pants back on, and step out into the hall empty-handed!' McGee's voice boomed in the small space. 'You've got one minute to come out, or I'll come in shootin'. You choose.'

McGee could hear curses emanate from the second room, while from the first came a crash, followed by a woman's scream. Then a voice called out from behind the first door, 'Hold your fire, I'm comin' out.'

'Which one are you?' McGee enquired, voice raised to be heard.

'Chance,' came the answer. 'I'm Chance.'

'Alright, come ahead. But you better be holdin' nothin' but air in your hands, or you're a dead man,' the bounty hunter warned.

The door creaked as it swung open on stiff hinges and revealed empty space.

'Are you comin' out?' McGee asked.

'Yeah, don't shoot,' came the urgent reply.

Chance McClane's frame filled the doorway, but he was holding a whore in front as a shield. The poor girl was frightened out of her skin, blue eyes wide with fear, while her scantily clad body shivered uncontrollably. Chance was partially clothed and wore only jeans.

'Here I am,' he said, his voice unusually loud.

It was a signal. The second door exploded outwards and Delbert McClane lunged through the opening with a blazing six-gun in his hand. Like his brother, the sandy-headed Delbert was half naked. His face was a screwed-up mask of hatred, and by the time he'd reached the center of the hallway, Delbert had fired three shots, all wild.

One gouged splinters from the plank paneled wall, while another blew a hole in the rear door behind McGee. The third shot came the closest, and clipped the bounty hunter's sleeve.

McGee stood calmly, squeezed the trigger, and the first barrel of the Greener fired. Its throaty roar filled the small space. The buckshot hit Delbert McClane square in the chest, blew him from his feet, and painted the hall with a fine spray of bright red blood.

'Delbert!' Chance cried in disbelief. 'You son of a bitch, you've killed him.'

From nowhere, Chance produced a Colt, and tried to line it up on McGee whilst struggling with the now-screaming whore.

Wolf McGee didn't hesitate. He casually aimed the shotgun at the pair and let loose with the last barrel. Once more, thunder filled the hallway as the charge of buckshot ripped apart everything in its path.

The whore's screams ceased abruptly as the lead balls took her in the throat and chest. The remaining lead shot peppered Chance and he collapsed to the floor, dragging the dead girl with him.

The barkeep appeared in the hall behind McGee. 'Maybelle! Damn you, mister, you've killed her.'

He pushed roughly past the bounty hunter, knelt down beside Maybelle, and cradled her head in his lap. 'You murdered her. I told you to be careful.'

'She got in the way,' the bounty hunter said callously. Then he leant down, grabbed Chance McClane by his hair, and began to drag him outside.

*   *   *

Three days later, Wolf McGee was in Twin Rocks to collect his bounty money.

'Eight hundred, nine hundred, one thousand.' The sheriff finished counting the notes and pointed at the paper on his scarred desk. 'Just sign here and you can leave.'

McGee signed in silence; once he'd finished, the sheriff, with contempt in his voice, said, 'Good. Now get on your horse and get out of my town.'

The bounty hunter sighed. 'Now, Sheriff, that ain't real friendly of you.'

'Friendly be damned,' he snorted. 'I've heard about you, McGee, and your methods. Frankly, I'd call you nothing more than a glorified killer. Now, take your money and get.'

Once outside, McGee stood on the scuffed boardwalk. Not yet decided whether to follow the sheriff's directions, he noticed a small, almost bald man hurrying along the street towards him. In his hand, he held a folded piece of paper.

'Excuse me, sir, are you Mister McGee?' he asked in a high-pitched voice.

'Who wants to know?'

'I'm O'Malley. I run the telegraph office. If you are Wolf McGee, then this is for you.' O'Malley held the paper up.

The bounty hunter nodded. 'I'm him.'

O'Malley gave him the creased note,

then stood and waited patiently.

'Was there anythin' else?' McGee asked him.

'Well, no . . . ' O'Malley smiled awkwardly. 'It's just that most folks give me a little something for my time, if you know what I mean?'

The bounty hunter gave him a cold look. 'Well, I ain't most folks.'

The telegraphist turned, his shoulders slumped, and walked off. Meanwhile, Wolf McGee unfolded the note and read:

GO TO GOLD CREEK STOP JOB FOR YOU STOP WILL PAY TOP DOLLAR STOP JOSHUA BELL UNITED STATES SECRET SERVICE.

Well, at least McGee knew what he was going to do next.

* * *

'Hey Cronk, what are you doin' sittin' up on this damn hill?' young Smitty asked.

'Just lookin', Smitty, just lookin'.'

Walter Cronkite, a veteran at fifty years, was solidly built and hard as nails. His face showed his age, but the deep-set brown eyes were as good as they'd ever been, and took in everything around them out of habit. Cronkite's clothes fit his job. Once a hardened gunfighter, he was now foreman of the K-Bar ranch.

In the last eight years, the only time Cronkite had drawn his Colt six-gun was to practice or to shoot snakes. His past was just that, and he was determined to leave it there.

'What do you want, Smitty?' he asked.

'Salty was in town pickin' up supplies this mornin', and the feller at the telegraph office gave him a wire for you.'

Smitty held it out to Cronkite, who in turn moved his sorrel forward and accepted the proffered sheet of paper, unfolded it, and read:

NEED YOUR HELP STOP COME TO GOLD CREEK NEW MEXICO STOP

WILL PAY FIVE THOUSAND DOLLARS
STOP JOSHUA BELL

Cronkite's brow furrowed. Who in hell was Joshua Bell? And what did he want?

He folded the paper and put it into the pocket of his faded blue shirt.

'Is everythin' alright Cronk?'

Cronkite nodded. 'Yeah Smitty, it's fine. You'd best be gettin' back.'

'Sure.' The young man swung his bay around and loped off down the slope, leaving the old gunfighter to himself.

Cronkite sat in his saddle and looked out across the valley at a line of cattle following the bank of the river that wound its way between the cotton-woods like a watery serpent. Quite often he would come here to admire the view across the valley and its lush grazing land. Which was more than most other men in his previous profession could do.

Somehow, he had been tracked down. After eight years of peace, the gun was calling his name once more.

Cronkite kept telling himself that he was too old and slow for gun work anymore, but the small shiver of fear was overwhelmed by the thrill of anticipation. He drew his Colt and checked the loads as he'd done countless times before, then slid it back in the holster. He knew exactly what he was going to do.

3

The Apache called it *Litsu tu*, Yellow Water. When the white men arrived, they named it Gold Creek.

It was just a shallow waterway, like many others, except for the yellow sands of the creek bed. When the sunlight hit it at a certain angle, the creek turned a brilliant shimmering gold color.

Since those early days, Gold Creek had been transformed into a bustling town with a population of four hundred citizens and many thriving businesses. Kinane rode his mustang across a solid timber bridge and into a main street full of false-front shops and intermittent adobe structures. It was morning, the sun sat like a round ball of fire in the clear blue sky, and storekeepers scuttled like a small army of ants, armed with straw brooms as they swept away the dust from the boardwalk at the front of their establishments. Nearby, a blacksmith hammered rhythmically, and the sound of metal on metal echoed in the clear morning air.

About two thirds of the way along the street, Kinane found what he was looking for. The small livery stable was set back from the main street, and had a sign above two large red doors that read 'Eli's Livery'.

Kinane eased his mustang up to the open doors and dismounted. The scent of fresh straw drifted out and masked any other odors that may have been present. As he stood and peered inside, he could see a line of stalls down both side walls, and an opening at the far end that framed a large corral out the back with a couple of horses in it.

'Hello, anybody there?' Kinane called loudly.

'Up here stranger,' a voice replied.

He looked up and spied the owner of the voice standing at the edge of the hayloft, holding a pitchfork. He was dressed in coveralls with flecks of straw hanging from him.

'I was wantin' to put my horse up for the night, maybe two,' explained Kinane.

'Hold on mister, I'll be right down.'

The hostler set aside the fork and climbed down a rickety ladder. He was a middle-aged man with streaky grey hair and a face wrinkled and worn by time. His wiry frame was starting to stoop from years of challenging work, but his brown eyes were full of life.

He smiled at Kinane and held out a friendly hand. 'Name's Eli, friend.'

Kinane took his callused hand and returned his firm grip. 'Kinane.'

'Say, seems to me I've heard of you.'

He ignored the man's comment. 'Can I leave my horse and gear here?'

'Sure, sure. No problems there. I have an empty stall four down on the right,' Eli paused before he asked, 'How long were you wantin' it for again?'

'A day, maybe two. I'm not certain.'

Eli followed Kinane who led his mustang past the stalls until he found the empty one. Kinane finished with the saddle and sat it on the wall of the Mustang's stall.

'Where's a good place to stay in town?'

'Depends on what your taste is,' Eli answered. 'The Gold Bullet saloon has rooms. Find yourself some company there as well. Might be a little noisy, though.'

'What else is there?'

Eli scratched at his head thoughtfully. 'Well, apart from two other saloons, there's Ma Richies' boardin' house and two hotels. Both on Main.'

Kinane nodded his thanks, dug into a pocket, and found a five-dollar gold piece. He flipped it to the hostler. 'I might try one of those. Will that cover the horse for a while?'

Eli looked at the coin. 'Sure will, and then some.'

Without another word Kinane draped his saddlebags over his shoulder, pulled the Winchester '76 from the saddle boot, and walked out into the bright sunlight.

The Grand Palace Hotel was a double-story concern with a neatly painted white facade and large glazed windows in the second-floor rooms. When Kinane opened the timber-and-glass door that led into the main foyer, a small bell was tripped and its jingling message filled the air.

A small balding man with spectacles emerged from a back room and greeted the gunfighter as he reached the counter.

'Can I help you, sir?' he asked pleasantly.

'I'm after a room,' Kinane informed him.

The clerk looked him up and down before he suggested apprehensively, 'Umm, might you be more comfortable at one of the saloons, sir?'

Kinane stared at the man but remained silent.

The clerk fidgeted uncomfortably with his string tie for a moment, then sighed, 'No, no; I don't expect you will be.'

He turned away and took down a key from a rusted hook on the wall. Turning back, he handed it to Kinane and gave him directions. 'Room seventeen. It's up the stairs, turn right, and you'll find it halfway along on the right. It overlooks Main Street. I hope it will be acceptable.'

'It'll be fine,' Kinane told him.

'If you will just sign the book, the room will be two dollars a night.'

Kinane signed the register with an almost illegible scrawl, but the clerk made out the name. 'Thank you, Mister Kinane.'

The man paused, deep in thought, and then: 'Ah, Mister Kinane. I have a note for you. A man left it here just in case you came in. I have it right here.'

The clerk ducked down below the polished counter, causing Kinane's right hand to drop to the butt of the Colt. You could never be too careful. The man emerged holding an envelope. 'There you are.'

Kinane took the note and said, 'Thank you, Mister . . . ?'

'Merriweather, Augustus Merriweather.'

Kinane nodded. 'Thank you Mister Merriweather.'

The gunfighter turned away and climbed the steps with the hand-carved balustrade. He turned right at the top of the stairs and walked along the hall until he found his room.

The room was small and tidy. Kinane placed his saddlebags on the iron-framed bed and leant the Winchester up against the hardwood dresser.

He opened the envelope, took out the piece of paper, unfolded it, and began to read:

COME TO THE GOLDEN WATERS HOTEL AT SIX. ASK FOR JOSHUA BELL.

There was that name again. Joshua Bell. A man he'd never heard of until recently. The meeting could be a setup or it may be legitimate. One thing was certain: if it was trouble, Kinane would be prepared.

★　★　★

The Golden Waters Hotel was the best place in town to stay by a long shot. As far as frontier hotels went, this one was luxurious.

The reception area had carpet, hand-carved ornaments, a chandelier, wood paneling, and a long mahogany counter. The staircase was made from redwood and there were polished brass knobs on the posts of the hand-tooled balustrade.

The man who stood behind the counter was impeccably dressed in a black suit and bow tie. He stared at Kinane for a moment before he spoke. 'You'd be here to see Mister Bell, sir. Am I right?'

The gunfighter was about to reply when the clerk cut him off. 'It's alright, sir, you are not the first gentleman to call on Mister Bell tonight.'

'So where can I find him?' asked Kinane.

'Why, in the suite of course, sir.'

'Of course,' Kinane muttered with more than a hint of sarcasm, 'but being a stranger to such a fine establishment as this, where might I find the suite?'

A shocked and embarrassed realization dawned on the clerk. 'Oh yes, sir. Sorry, sir. If you go up the stairs and turn to your left, then go along the hallway, you will find the suite at the end of the corridor.'

Kinane touched the brim of his Stetson. 'Much obliged.'

After following the directions he'd been given, Kinane stopped at a dark timber door, then rapped loudly with his knuckles.

'Enter,' came a muffled voice from the other side.

As he dropped his left hand to the knob, Kinane's first instinct was to unhook the hammer thong from the Colt with his right and kept his hand resting on the gun butt. Only then did he twist the knob and give the door a little shove so that it swung open freely.

Kinane braced himself, in anticipation of the bullet he expected to come. Instead, a man appeared in the doorway and motioned for him to enter.

As Kinane stepped warily across the threshold, his eyes swept the room and took in the four people present as the man introduced himself. 'I'm Joshua Bell. You have to be either Smith or Kinane, as everybody else is here already.'

'He's Kinane,' a familiar voice answered. Seated in a corner in a high-backed chair, as large as life, was Walter Cronkite.

'Howdy Cronk, it's been a while.'

The old gunfighter smiled warmly. 'Sure has, kid; how you been keepin'?'

'Can't complain. Still breathin'; that's somethin', I suppose.'

Cronkite nodded. 'Yeah kid, I hear what you're sayin'.'

'Well, isn't this nice,' said a voice that dripped with sarcasm. 'A family reunion. You all better stop now before I go and get all warm and fuzzy.'

Kinane turned to face the man who stood next to the sideboard. Hawk's appearance had changed some since he'd been freed from prison. His brown hair was neatly trimmed and his face was clean-shaven. The prison garb was gone, and he was now wearing his familiar black attire. Around his waist was his silver studded double gun-rig with twin Colts, grips inlaid with silver hawks.

Cronkite broke the uneasy silence. 'You'll stand down, Hawk, if you know what's good for you.'

Hawk shifted his cold gaze to the old gunfighter. 'Why might that be, old man? Just because you say so?'

'He's too good for you, Hawk,' Cronkite declared, 'that is my say-so.'

'What would you know?' Hawk snapped venomously.

'I know because I taught him. He's better than I ever was. He's that damned good.'

Hawk smiled coldly. 'I guess we'll find out before this is over.'

Kinane's face remained impassive as he said, 'How about we find out now?'

The room was deathly silent as the challenge hung heavily in the air. Now it was up to Hawk.

The killer shook his head. 'No, I think this can wait until later. Get this job done and then I can kill you with a clean slate.'

Kinane let his eyes drift across to McGee, who stood silently smiling as he stood near the window. His gaze lingered on him, and then switched back to Hawk.

'Well, gentlemen . . . ' Bell said to ease the tension. 'Now that you've got that out of the way, Mister Kinane, would you like something to drink?'

'Not just yet, Mister Bell — there's one more thing.'

Bell gave the gunfighter a questioning look. 'What might that be?'

'Did you see it, Cronk?' Kinane asked the old gunfighter.

He nodded. 'Yeah kid, I saw it.'

'Mister Bell, tell your man on the other side of that bedroom door to put up that shotgun he has poked through the crack and step out here,' Kinane ordered, 'or I'm goin' to put some lead through it.'

Bell realized what the gunfighter was talking about and smiled warily. He called towards the door, 'Jess, come on out and meet these fine gentlemen.'

The door swung wide and out walked the shotgun holder.

'Gentlemen, meet Jess Stuart.'

All the gunmen froze, their mouths wide. Before them, dressed in jeans, cotton shirt and a tied-down holster full of single-action Remington, was a woman.

She was slim, but her curves were accentuated by the fitted clothes. Jess's olive-colored face was framed by long black hair; her eyes were brown, and her lips were full.

While Hawk and McGee ogled the newcomer, Kinane stared into her eyes. Between them and the firm set of her jaw, he could tell she possessed a steely resolve that a lot of men lacked.

'Jess will be going with you,' Bell announced.

'The hell you say,' said Hawk.

'Hold on a damn minute,' Cronk

protested. 'We don't yet have an idea where we are goin', but if you think she's goin' anywhere with this bunch, think again.'

'Ease up a minute, Cronk,' Kinane soothed, 'let's hear the man out. I have a hunch the lady can take care of herself.'

The old gunfighter hesitated briefly before muttering, 'Well, alright. We'll listen.'

'*Listen* be damned!' It was Hawk's turn to have his say. 'Just because she's got a gun strapped on don't make her any less of a woman.'

'So, what's your point?' Jess asked.

'My point is, you ain't goin'. Wherever *it* is. And judging by the bunch in this here room, it's goin' to be too blamed dangerous to have a woman taggin' along, and I ain't goin' to be playin' nursemaid to you.'

Jess pursed her lips, and stared hard into Hawk's eyes. Suddenly her shoulder dipped and her hand came up full of cocked Remington.

Hawk was taken completely by surprise.

'I can nursemaid myself,' Jess said evenly.

Cronkite laughed out loud. 'You know what, kid? I think I like her already.'

Kinane nodded. 'Startin' to grow on me some, too.'

'Gentlemen you'll find Jessie most capable,' Bell explained with a certain pride. 'She is one of my best agents. You see, we both work for the United States Secret Service.'

There was a knock on the door, and it swung open to reveal a man in his forties. His salt-and-pepper hair and his heavily lined face were signs of his age. His broad shoulders sat square; hidden beneath the grey cotton shirt he wore were numerous scars from bullet and blade.

'You would be Utah Smith?' asked Bell and stepped towards the famous town-tamer.

It was a statement, not a question,

and the man answered, 'I am.'

'Good, that means you are all here. I'm Joshua Bell. Mister Smith, if you'll have a seat, we'll get started.'

4

'Four weeks ago,' Bell began, 'United States Senator Phineas Sugden, and his wife and daughter, were in Rivertown, here in New Mexico. It is a town some forty miles from here. They were there for the twenty-five-year anniversary. Things were going smoothly until a band of Mexican bandits rode into town. They slaughtered most of the population and took the senator and his family. According to the survivors, the senator appeared to be the target of the raid.'

'I'm guessin',' Cronkite interrupted, 'that the kidnapping is money-driven.'

Bell nodded. 'It would seem that way. They have asked for a ransom of one hundred thousand dollars.'

The group digested the information.

'Wait a minute.' This time it was Utah Smith who spoke up. 'You mean to say that them bandits took a U.S.

senator and only asked for a hundred thousand dollars?'

'That's about it,' Bell confirmed.

Utah was confused. 'But why? I mean, they could have asked for five times that much and got it.'

'We're not sure, but we think it is because they are not really bandits. They're Mexican rurales.'

'So why ain't the cavalry goin' after them?' Kinane asked.

'The government isn't willing to start another Mexican war,' Bell explained, 'which would happen if a cavalry troop crossed the border. It would not matter about the senator and his family, it would just be viewed as an act of aggression.'

'So, you want us to cross the border and bring them back,' concluded Hawk.

'In a way, yes.' Bell nodded and then continued. 'Gentlemen, I have spent countless hours sending out wires across territories and states to track you down because it is my belief that you are best qualified for this job. If you accept this assignment you will be paid five thousand dollars for your troubles.'

'Keep talkin' then, Bell, so we can make a decision,' Kinane told the secret service man.

Bell went on. 'So, you know where the senator was taken from. Now, from eyewitness reports, we believe that the man who has him is called Jesus Mendoza.'

'I've heard of him,' Wolf McGee informed the group. 'I chased a feller name of Mesquite Jones across the border last spring. South of the Big Bend country. I followed him to a small village a half-day ride south of the Rio. By the time I arrived, Mendoza had already found him. He was hangin' naked from a frame in the town square. They'd flogged him to death. He's mean, that one.'

Bell nodded. 'Yes, quite. From what we know of him, he's a cold-blooded killer.'

'So where do we find him?' asked Cronkite.

'A village called Las Palomas.'

'That's the place,' interjected McGee.

'The village is small, but is used as a rurale outpost,' Bell explained.

'What else?' asked Kinane.

Bell shrugged. 'That's about it.'

'That's mighty thin, Bell.'

'Yes, it is,' the man agreed. 'You will have to assess the situation when you arrive.'

'What about her?'

All turned their attention towards Hawk. He held up a hand placatingly. 'Before you all get bent out of shape, just listen for a moment. If you dress her in some female clothes and dirty her face a little, with her hair all hangin' down she could pass as a Mexican woman.'

Bell started to object, but Cronkite stopped him. 'It makes sense. What do you think, kid?'

'It could work,' Kinane allowed, 'but it don't matter much what I think. The question is, would Jessie be willin' to do it?'

'I can do it,' she said confidently.

'How's your Spanish?'

'I get by.'

'Alright then.'

'There is something else,' Bell declared.

'What?' asked Kinane.

The government man gestured to a battered trunk in the far corner of the room. 'In that, you will find one hundred thousand dollars. You are to take it with you.'

After a long silence, Kinane was the first to express his concerns and opinion about Bell's announcement. 'Are you crazy? You don't just take that much money into Mexico. Every two-bit bandit between here and Mexico City will be huntin' us.'

'I assure you,' Bell said calmly, 'that we in this room are the only ones who know about it.'

Kinane shook his head. 'That's just it. It won't be just us. Things like this have a way of getting out. By the time we cross the border, half the territory will know.'

'Surely you exaggerate,' the government man said, dismissing the claims.

'I guess we'll find out, won't we?' Cronkite said.

Meanwhile, Hawk stood quietly as his mind worked overtime. One hundred thousand dollars sure was a lot of money. Wolf McGee thought the same thing.

Utah Smith asked, 'Who's goin' to be leadin' this expedition?'

'Kinane,' Bell said authoritatively. 'He'll be in charge. What he says goes. Will there be a problem with that?'

'No,' Smith answered.

'I have a problem with that.' Hawk stated.

Bell sighed impatiently. 'What is your problem, Mister Hawk?'

'If I go, I ain't takin' orders from him or anybody else.'

'You have two choices, Mister Hawk,' Bell said as he laid it out clearly for the killer. 'You can go and follow orders, or you go back to prison. Your choice.'

Hawk's hand dropped threateningly to the butt of one of his six-guns. 'The hell I will.'

The secret service agent was unmoved by the killer's open challenge. 'Yes you will, Mister Hawk.'

Hawk began to slowly and deliberately draw one of his Colts.

'Now, before you go and do something that we may both regret, think about this. You may kill me Mister Hawk,' Bell said coolly, 'but do you think you will get out of this room alive before you are shot down? Trust me, if you don't do as you are asked, you will go back to prison.'

Rage burned in Hawk's eyes, but he let the gun drop back into its holster and hissed, 'Alright. I'll go.'

As the tension in the room eased, Kinane, Jessie and Utah let their hands fall away from their guns. Cronkite, however, made a clear display of letting the hammer down and reholstering his.

Bell turned his attention to Kinane. 'When will you leave?'

'In the mornin',' the gunfighter said.

'Fine. That will be all, gentlemen.'

Before Kinane could make a move towards the door, the government man blocked his path. 'Could you, Mister Cronkite and Jessie remain behind for a moment, please?'

Kinane looked across at his friend,

and Cronkite shrugged his shoulders.

'Sure, why not,' answered Kinane, a little curious.

After the others had left, Joshua Bell explained his actions. 'I asked you to stay behind because, quite frankly, I do not trust the others. You know about Hawk and McGee, but I am unsure about Smith.'

'From what I've heard about Smith, he's pretty much straight up,' Kinane assured him.

'Well, why bring them in on it?' asked Cronkite a little puzzled.

'Because they get the job done,' Kinane supplied the answer. 'Killers, but good.'

Bell agreed. 'Correct.'

'So why trust us?' the gunfighter asked. 'We're just as much killers as what they are.'

'No, Mister Kinane: even though you both live and die by the same sword, you are completely different beasts. No offence.'

'None taken.'

Bell walked across to the chest. 'As for the money . . . '

He took a key from his pocket, unlocked the lock and lifted the lid. The two gunmen and Jessie moved forward and peered in. No one said a word.

Bell locked it back up and faced the three. He gave the key to Kinane. 'You'd best bury it when you get across the border. With it being the only bargaining chip you have, you don't want to lose it.'

Kinane nodded grimly.

'Don't use it unless you have to.'

'Anythin' else?'

'No.'

'Good. Come on, Cronk, I'm hungry. Let's go eat.'

'Do you want some company?' Jessie asked.

Kinane shrugged. 'Sure, why not?'

* * *

'You know the whole thing is crazy, right?' Kinane said as he slopped up the last of his gravy with a piece of bread.

'I know why I'm goin',' said Cronkite. 'What about you?'

'Money, same as you.'

'What about you, Jessie?' Cronkite asked as he turned his attention towards the woman. 'Why are you goin'?'

'It's my job,' she answered.

'No,' the old gunfighter pointed out, 'this is most likely a one-way trip.'

Jessie took a sip of her coffee and placed the still-half-full cup back on the table. She shifted the focus of the conversation back to Cronkite. 'What about you? Kinane says it's the money, but if you'll excuse me for saying so, there has to be an easier way for a man your age to earn it.'

Cronkite smiled broadly. 'Did you hear that, kid? The young lady is tellin' me I'm too old and should be livin' out my days in a rockin' chair on some front porch.'

Jessie's face colored a bright shade of red. 'No, that's not what I was saying.'

Kinane smiled.

'Hell, I know that, girl!' Cronkite burst out laughing and relieved some of Jessie's embarrassment. 'If you did, you would probably be right. This is a young man's game. But if I had a choice, I'd rather go out facin' a smokin' Colt than rockin' myself to death.'

Jessie turned her attention to Kinane. 'What about you? Why do you do it?'

The smile vanished from Kinane's face. 'You ask too many questions.'

With that, he stood abruptly and stalked out of the café.

Jessie was taken aback and shot Cronk a concerned look. 'I didn't mean to upset him. I guess it's working as an agent, you kind of get used to asking questions.'

'Don't worry about it, Jessie,' the old gunfighter tried to soothe her distress, 'it's not you. He's like a lot of gunmen who have their own demons to deal with.'

'What do you mean?'

Cronkite sighed, 'In another life,

Kinane had himself a family, a wife and child. They had a small farm in Texas. They were livin' happily, doin' their own thing, until it changed overnight.'

Cronkite took a sip of his coffee before he continued. 'A bunch of outlaws came through one night, on the run from a posse that were chasin' them. They'd robbed a bank in a small town fifty miles or so north. They had been ridin' hard and needed fresh mounts. They jumped Kinane outside and knocked him cold. When he came to, the outlaws were gone and his house was burned to the ground. His wife and little girl were inside when they done it.'

The expression on Jessie's face was one of sadness more than one of shock. 'How awful for him.'

The old gunfighter nodded. 'When I found him, he was on foot trackin' them killers. All he had was a knife and a world of hate to keep him goin'. So, I helped him out. Gave him a spare gun that I carried and showed him how to use it properly. Funny thing, though, the kid was a natural. He could clear leather as fast as any man I'd seen, includin' me. I offered to help him out by goin' with him. After all, there were six of them. But he wouldn't hear of it and we parted ways right there, him still on foot.'

Cronkite paused and retrieved his tobacco pouch from his jacket pocket. 'Mind if I smoke, ma'am?'

'No, but you can stop callin' me ma'am and call me Jessie.'

The old gunfighter nodded and rolled his cigarette, put it in the corner of his mouth and lit it. He blew out a cloud of blue-grey smoke and said, 'Now, where was I?'

'Kinane had just left you.'

'That's right,' he said. 'I never saw him for close on two years after that. He'd caught up with them outlaws and they'd all paid for what they done. Ever since then, he's been usin' his gun to go up against bad men. Always hires out on the side of good. I guess he figures the more bad men he kills, the less likelihood there'll be of somethin' happenin' to somebody else the way it was done to him.'

'It's sad that a man could be changed so much like that,' Jessie observed.

'Don't misjudge him, Jessie. Deep down, that same feller is still there. Kinane just keeps him locked away. Maybe someday, if he finds the right woman again, he might emerge.'

Jessie stayed quiet. She sat there and looked at the empty doorway.

5

As he walked along the dimly lit boardwalk, Kinane was softly cursing himself for being so short with Jessie. It wasn't her fault that questions irritated him so.

Maybe it was the job. He sure as hell wasn't over the moon about taking her along. But she was going, and that was that.

Kinane walked slowly, the heels of his boots making a clunking sound in the still night air every time he placed one down on the scarred and worn planks. The night was cool and crisp, and a big silver moon hung suspended in the cloudless sky, stars provided a sparkling backdrop for the large pockmarked orb.

The gunfighter came to an intersection and stepped down into the street. No sooner had his foot touched its hard-packed dusty surface than a rifle shot whiplashed and the muzzle flame briefly illuminated where the bush-whacker had staked out.

Kinane felt the bullet fan his face. The heat of its passing almost scorched the skin of his cheek.

He palmed up his Colt, moved quickly for the cover of two water barrels, and fired two shots in the direction of the muzzle flash as he went. Another shot came from the darkened laneway opposite. This time, the flame illuminated the figure of a man crouched down on one knee against the side of a building.

Kinane fired in his general direction, hoping to score a lucky hit. The killer answered with two more shots. One gouged a chunk of wood from the side of a barrel which caused a torrent of water to pour out. The other whined low overhead and caused Kinane to instinctively duck down.

The gunfighter loosed three more shots in swift succession and dropped back down behind cover. Kinane opened the loading gate on the Colt and let the empty casings fall to the dirt. He swiftly thumbed in fresh bullets and was once again ready to continue the fight.

More shots came from across the street, and sharp wooden splinters sliced through the air. The shooter had changed his position in the laneway, utilizing the cover of darkness to mask his movements.

Kinane thought for a moment then clenched his jaw in grim determination. He stood erect, and presented the bushwhacker with a clear target. So, eager was the killer that his shot came too quickly and the bullet flew wide.

Kinane returned fire, this time with all six shots that the Colt's chambers housed. With every squeeze of the trigger the six-gun bucked, and after each event, the gunfighter shifted his aim fractionally until the shots had been evenly spaced out across the laneway. His gun empty once more, Kinane dropped behind cover once more to reload.

With the echoes of the shots dying away from around the rooftops of the town, Kinane thought that he heard a muffled curse. He waited for the bushwhacker to fire again, but the laneway opposite remained quiet.

Kinane stood up cautiously. Nothing happened.

Suddenly the night was filled with angry shouts, and he turned to look down Main Street. A crowd had gathered, and like an encroaching tide was headed in his direction. Leading the pack was a man with a shotgun, and Kinane caught the flicker of light reflected from a badge pinned to his chest.

The crowd stopped and the sheriff stepped forward.

'What the hell is goin' on here, stranger?' he asked angrily.

Kinane holstered his Colt and glanced at the hostile-looking crowd that backed the sheriff. Amongst them he saw a pair of friendly faces, Cronkite and Jessie.

He turned his attention back to the lawman. The sheriff was a middle-aged man, well-built and tall, and had an air of confidence about him that came only with experience.

'I asked you a question, mister?'

'Someone from across the street started shootin' at me,' Kinane answered honestly.

'And?'

'I shot back.'

'Did you happen to see who it was?' the lawman asked.

'Nope, it was too dark.'

The sheriff called back over his shoulder, 'A couple of you fellers go and check out that laneway across the street, and see if this trigger-happy ranny is tellin' the truth.'

Kinane watched as two men peeled away from the crowd, closely followed by Cronkite. The three of them disappeared into the alley, and after a couple of minutes the two townsmen reemerged.

'Well, what did you find?' the sheriff asked impatiently.

'We didn't find nothin', Mort. The laneway was empty,' answered a short, thin man. 'Whoever was there sure ain't now. But there was someone. The smell of gunsmoke is still lingerin' in the air.'

The sheriff looked at Kinane, contempt etched on his face. 'So, maybe what you said was true. But tomorrow you are gone from here. Your kind only bring trouble to towns like ours.'

With that, the sheriff spun on his heel and stalked off, the crowd following him.

Kinane was left standing in the street with Cronkite and Jessie.

'Are you alright, kid?' the old gunfighter asked.

'Yeah, I'm fine.'

'Are you sure?' asked Jessie.

'Stop fussin', it ain't like I've never been shot at before.' He brushed the concern aside then asked Cronkite, 'You found nothin' at all?'

'Not exactly. I found this,' the old gunfighter said holding out a folded piece of paper.

A puzzled Kinane unfolded it and

held the sheet of paper just right so the dim light of a lantern enabled him to read it.

WANTED FOR MURDER!
RED KINANE
FOR THE COLD-BLOODED MURDER OF
KENO BLAINE
$10,000 REWARD (DEAD)
BRING BODY TO FLYING SPUR RANCH

Kinane looked at Cronkite and then at Jessie.

'Someone sure as hell wants you dead, kid,' the old gunman observed.

Kinane nodded. 'So it would seem.'

'I'll only ask you once, kid; did you do what it says?'

'No.' Kinane went on to tell them both about his previous job.

'He sure didn't take long to get them printed and distributed,' Cronkite said.

Jessie held out her hand. 'Give it to me.'

'Why?'

'I can take it to Bell and he can do

60

something about it,' she explained.

Kinane passed her the wanted dodger.

'One more thing,' she said. 'About before . . . '

'Forget about it.' Kinane stopped her. 'It was more my doin' than yours.'

Jessie walked off and left the two men standing in the street. Kinane looked at his friend. 'You told her, didn't you?'

'Sure did.'

*   *   *

Somewhere a rooster crowed as the sun slowly clawed its way above the mountains to the west. Kinane's horse stomped the hard-packed earth and snorted great gusts of breath, keen to be on the trail.

Hawk, Wolf McGee, Utah Smith and Jessie sat saddle, waiting for Kinane and Cronkite, who were off a way talking to Bell.

'Are you sure you can do somethin' about them?' the gunfighter asked

Bell nodded. 'Don't worry about them. I'll send off some wires and get it done. Should be fixed by the time you're back across the river.'

'What about the man who posted the reward?' Kinane asked.

'I'll send some agents to have a word with him. If he doesn't see reason, they'll lock him away for hiring assassins. Should get fifteen to life for that.'

Kinane stuck out his hand. 'Thanks, Bell; appreciate it.'

'Just bring Jessie back to me in one piece,' the government man said. 'I'd hate to lose such a good agent.'

'One thing is for certain, Mister Bell,' Cronkite put in, 'if she don't come back, we won't be back either.'

'That, Mister Cronkite, is a real possibility.'

'Come on, Cronk, let's go,' said Kinane.

'I'll see you in Redemption, Texas,' Bell called after them.

A few minutes later, the small band

rode out of Gold Creek. Utah Smith and the bounty hunter McGee brought up the rear, leading the two pack animals. One had supplies that Bell had organized, and the other carried the chest.

★　★　★

Six riders, six guns, heading south. How many would return was yet to be determined.

6

Desert country. Everywhere you looked the landscape was covered in yucca, creosote, mesquite, prickly pear and sand, all-enveloped in an unforgiving heat. Five riders, riding in single file, traversed this harsh terrain. The sixth, Hawk, was scouting a mile or so ahead of the small column.

Cronkite eased his horse out of line and rode towards Kinane out front. As the old gunfighter passed Utah Smith, the town-tamer asked in a casual voice, 'You see 'em?'

'Yeah,' was all Cronkite said as he kept moving.

He passed Jessie and finally fell in beside Kinane.

'What's up?' Kinane asked Cronkite.

'You know we're bein' followed, right?'

'Yeah,' Kinane answered without

looking back. 'I've been tryin' to work out how many there are.'

'There's four that I could see,' Cronkite informed him.

'Are you sure?'

Cronkite snorted, 'Damn, kid; I may be gettin' old, but I ain't blind.'

Kinane smiled faintly.

'What do you want to do?' the old gunfighter asked him.

Kinane shrugged. 'Keep ridin', I guess, see what plays out.'

'Could be worse, I suppose,' Cronkite surmised. 'It might have been Indians. But I hope they make their move sooner rather than later. Havin' them back there bird-doggin' us makes me nervous.'

With that, the old gunfighter pulled his horse up and waited for the others to ride past before taking his place at the tail of the column.

*　*　*

Cronkite was right. There were four men or, rather, three men and a kid.

Bell, Wright and Johnstone were full-time drifters and part-time outlaws who crossed the line when the need arose.

The kid, on the other hand, considered himself hell on wheels, and had already started to carve notches into the grips of his six-gun: a nickel-plated, pearl-handled Colt .45. Like other would-be gunhands, he was slow, and his conquests were all cow-punchers who used their guns to shoot snakes, not start up gunfights.

'Let's go down there and get 'em,' he crowed enthusiastically as the four lay watching from a low saddle between two hills.

'Shut up Lawrence,' whispered Bell harshly.

'Yeah Lawrence, shut up,' echoed Wright.

'I told you fellers not to call me that,' the young man hissed. 'Call me Kid.'

There was silence before the Kid spoke again.

'Let me at him,' he bragged. 'I can take him, I know it.'

'There just ain't nothin' between those damn ears of yours, is there, Kid?' Johnstone said gruffly. 'Any one of those riders down there would chew you up and spit you out in pieces. Besides, you already tried it and it damn near got you killed.'

'I could have had him with your help,' he protested.

'We don't go in for bushwhackin'. Now shut up.'

'What do you think?' Wright asked Bell.

'We'll do it after sundown. They'll be wore out from the day's ride and not expectin' trouble.'

They all nodded in agreement. The Kid tapped the flyer in his breast pocket. By this time tomorrow, they would be on their way to collect ten thousand dollars.

★   ★   ★

'They're out there alright.' Smith spoke in hushed tones as he moved into the firelight. 'They're movin' in slowly, tryin' to be quiet.'

'How long before they'll be in position?' Kinane asked.

Utah shrugged. 'The way them hombres are movin', maybe half an hour.'

Cronkite nodded. 'Let's get ready, then.'

'Leave the chest out in the open,' ordered Kinane.

They went about preparing for their expected guests, except for Hawk. He sat off to one side, brooding, planning.

'Are you goin' to do somethin'?' asked Cronkite.

Hawk looked at him coldly. 'I'll shoot someone when the time comes.'

'In the back?'

Hawk's hand moved towards his Colt.

'Pull that gun and I'll kill you,' warned Kinane.

Hawk stayed his hand and turned his head. He stared into the barrel of Kinane's six-gun. 'You've been told, Hawk, I won't tell you again.'

'Get one thing straight, Kinane,'

Hawk hissed, his eyes blazing with fury. 'I don't like you, and I'm only here 'cause I have to be. Once this thing is done, there's goin' to be a reckonin'.'

'I won't be too hard to locate.'

Hawk rose and stalked off into the darkness.

'Watch yourself, kid; he'll backshoot you, that one,' Cronkite cautioned.

'Do me a favor, Cronk, don't ride him so hard. We have all the trouble we need without addin' him to the mix.'

The old gunfighter nodded. 'Sure, kid, I'll do that.'

★　★　★

A voice came from the darkness that startled Hawk, and caused him to drop his hand to one of his guns and half-draw it.

'Havin' trouble?'

It was Wolf McGee.

'What's it to you?' Hawk snapped tersely.

'Nothin' to me.' The bounty hunter

shrugged his shoulders. 'But the way I see it, both you and me have got somethin' in common.'

Hawk waited for McGee to elaborate.

'We both want what's in that chest.'

'I'm listenin',' the killer said.

'I was thinkin' that you and me could team up and take that there box of money.'

'Maybe. I'll think about it.'

'Don't think too long, compadre.' McGee smiled slyly.

★   ★   ★

The four bushwhackers came upon the camp close to an hour later. They took their time, carefully picking a path through the clumps of prickly pear and rock. Somewhere out in the desert, a coyote yipped and then howled. A lonesome sound that drifted across the desert on a slight breeze.

They stopped and looked over the camp. The woman and the old man sat beside the campfire. The others were in their bedrolls, flames from the fire causing a flickering light to dance across their prone forms.

'Let's go,' Bell whispered. 'Don't shoot unless you have to. We only want one man.'

'The flyer said 'dead',' the Kid said in a muffled voice.

'Shut up, Kid,' hissed Wright.

'I'm not goin' to gun him cold,' stated Bell. 'Now, let's get it done.'

The four men stood, spread out, and walked into camp. Guns drawn, hammers back on full cock.

'Everybody stay right where you are,' Bell called loudly. 'We don't want to hurt anyone.'

Red Kinane casually walked out of the inky blackness on the other side of the fire. 'Sounds like good advice, mister. I think maybe you all should take it.'

Instantly, all four men grew nervous at the reality that they'd been outsmarted.

'Don't try anythin' silly. There's three guns out there in the darkness that have you covered,' Kinane warned. 'One wrong move and you'll be dead before you know it. Just drop your hardware, gents.'

Bell's shoulders slumped forward and he sighed with resignation. 'Hold your fire, you've got us. Throw 'em down, fellers.'

Bell, Wright and Johnstone dropped their weapons. They made dull thuds as they landed in the dirt.

'What about you, Kid?' Kinane's withering gaze only served to make the young man more nervous.

'Drop the damn gun, Kid,' Bell snapped.

The Kid licked his lips. His mouth was dry, but still he held his piece.

'Listen to him, Kid,' Kinane cautioned softly, 'you can still walk away from this.'

The Kid's last sense of self-preservation was telling him to drop his gun, but ten thousand dollars was a lot of money, and it was standing right in front of him not twenty feet distant. He hadn't come this far just to walk away.

'Kid!' Bell exclaimed.

The Kid started to move his gun through a short arc to line it up on the gunfighter.

With a hint of dismay, Kinane sighed. His shoulder dipped and before anyone could blink his Colt roared, an orange flame erupting from its barrel in the semi-darkness. He fired two shots before the Kid could even put pressure on the trigger.

Both slugs hit the Kid in the chest, and threw him back in the dirt.

'Oh hell!' cried Wright.

Before the rumbling echoes of the gunshots had died away, the night was filled with the roll of thunder once more. The three remaining men danced like marionettes as bullets from unseen rifles slammed into each of them.

Then, as suddenly as they'd begun, the rifles fell silent and all three men were down. Bell and Johnstone were dead, and Wright was dying.

Kinane cursed and knelt at Wright's side. Blood bubbled from his chest and he gasped for air as his lungs rapidly filled with blood.

'We . . . we were unarmed,' Wright gasped out, 'there . . . there was no . . . no need to shoot.'

Kinane's face remained grim as he crouched over the dying man. There was a gurgling sigh and Wright died.

Anger coursed through the gunfighter as he stood and turned his hostile gaze directly upon Hawk and McGee as they emerged from the darkness.

'You damned backshootin' murderin' sons of bitches, they were unarmed. They couldn't hurt anyone,' Kinane blazed.

'Call it what you want.' Hawk shrugged. 'It's done.'

'As far as we could tell from out there in the dark,' McGee explained, 'we saved your life.'

'Damn straight,' Hawk chorused. 'You should be thankin' us.'

Kinane stared at the pair, fighting

back the urge to kill them. Cronkite eased up beside him and spoke quietly. 'Let it go, kid. I don't agree with it either, but it's done. There'll be plenty of time to settle up after the job's finished.'

'Bury them,' Kinane snapped. 'All four of them.'

'Don't push me, Kinane,' Hawk said frostily.

'You heard the man, bury them,' Utah Smith ordered. Up until now he'd remained silent.

'You stay out of this, town-tamer,' McGee told Smith as he turned in his direction.

The bounty hunter pulled up short as he stared down the gaping barrel of Utah's Winchester.

'This ain't got nothin' to do with you, Smith,' Hawk said coolly. 'Like Wolf said, stay out of it.'

Utah shook his head. 'Nope, don't believe I can. Now, I ain't sayin' I like bushwhackers much; but backshooters who gun down unarmed men, that's somethin' else entirely. I'd like to hang the both of you.'

Hawk snorted. 'You was out there too, mister high-and-mighty.'

'I was,' Utah allowed, 'but I never fired a shot.'

As he finished his sentence, Smith tossed the rifle to Cronkite, who inspected it.

'He's right, it ain't been fired,' Cronkite acknowledged, and passed it back.

There was silence for a time before Hawk cursed. 'Alright, damn it, I'll bury your bodies.'

Kinane watched as Hawk and McGee dragged the dead men out into the desert to bury them. He then turned his attention to Jessie who had remained silent throughout it all.

'Are you okay?'

From beneath the blanket she had draped across her knees, Jessie produced her cocked Remington and let the hammer down. 'I'm fine, I'm a big girl.'

'Just checkin'.'

Cronkite approached the pair. 'I found this on the young 'un.'

Kinane took the flyer from the old gunfighter. 'Damn that man.'

'Yeah,' Cronkite agreed, 'I reckon the temptation was too much for the kid.'

Kinane screwed up the flyer and threw it in the fire, then called Utah Smith over. 'You take first watch. McGee can relieve you in a few hours.'

'Sure, no problem.'

'One more thing, Utah,' Kinane added. 'Watch your back from here on out.'

'Always do,' the town-tamer said.

7

The six riders stopped their horses atop a long ridgeline and looked down at the shimmering serpent that cut its way through the hostile landscape.

'Well, we made it this far,' Cronkite observed as he wiped his face. Dust had turned to small rivulets of fine mud from the sweat that ran down his skin. 'That's Mexico over there.'

Kinane called over to Wolf McGee, 'Give Hawk the pack horse. You ride scout from here on. Reckon you can find your way?'

'Do it with my eyes shut,' McGee answered.

The bounty hunter gave Hawk the lead rope and let his horse pick its way downslope towards the water.

They followed the river for a mile or so before they came across a ford. The steep river banks flattened out and the water shallowed enough for the horses to cross without any problems.

Once on the Mexican side, the riders followed the trail through steep-sided ravines and canyons until, finally, the trail opened out into the vast expanse of the desert country beyond.

A mile from the canyon country, McGee returned and told them that the trail ahead was clear.

Kinane nodded and decided on his next move. 'Right then, this will do.'

'Do for what?' McGee asked, confused.

'You'll see. Will we make Las Palomas tomorrow?'

'If we push it.'

'Fine, this will do.'

Kinane stopped the small column beside a boulder formation that stood high above the desert floor. They dismounted in the shadows and he called Jessie over. He pointed to a flat boulder protruding from the rock face. 'Can you climb up there and keep a lookout?'

'Sure.'

'Good, take your rifle and keep a

good eye out. The last thing we want is for a rurale patrol to jump us while we're buryin' the chest. If somethin' does happen, stay up there out of sight. I want to avoid trouble.'

Jessie smiled wryly. Her eyes sparkled and Red noticed how pretty she was under the dirt and grime on her face.

'Look around you.' She half-laughed. 'You're in Mexico with at least two men who want to kill you, you're riding into the lion's den, and you might never return. To top it off, you have ten thousand dollars on your head.'

Kinane smiled back. 'Alright, I could do without any more trouble. Satisfied?'

'You should do that more often.'

Kinane frowned. 'What?'

'Smile,' Jessie explained before she turned and walked away.

Kinane watched her go.

'What are we doin'?' Cronkite had slipped up beside him.

'We're goin' to bury that chest.'

'Thought so,' answered the old gun-fighter as he eyed Kinane watching Jessie.

'Whatever it is you're thinkin', kid, put it to one side now.'

Kinane turned and faced his friend. 'What do you mean?'

'Hell, we're ridin' into God knows what, and you need to be focused on how we're goin' to get back out.'

Cronkite turned away and left Kinane standing alone. He was right, but there was something about Jessie that reminded him of Mary. Unconsciously he reached into his pocket and felt for the small chain and crucifix. It was still there.

* * *

For almost an hour Jessie kept watch while the chest was being buried beneath the desert sands. She stared out across the harsh landscape marked with boulders, ocotillo and yucca, and noticed a vulture that soared high above the desert floor and the heat-haze that shimmered and rippled distorting the horizon.

The men were almost finished when Jessie noticed the dust cloud out in the dry wasteland. It started out faint, a smudge off in the distance whose density grew as it came closer. At the base of the cloud Jessie could finally make out the riders.

* * *

'Tell me why we're buryin' all this money way out here in the middle of nowhere,' Hawk griped.

'How long do you think we'll last, Hawk, if we ride in there totin' a hundred thousand in that damn chest?' Kinane's voice dripped with sarcasm.

Hawk remained silent.

Kinane was about to continue when a small rock plunged down from above.

'What the hell!' exclaimed Hawk.

Both men looked up and saw Jessie gesturing off to the southwest.

They looked out across the desert and saw the rising dust cloud roiling up into the sky.

'Damn, we got company,' Hawk cursed.

Kinane looked back up at Jessie and held his arms wide in a questioning gesture.

She signaled back, and from her motions he made out that there were six riders, all wearing big hats.

Bandits, thought Kinane. Damn it to hell. He gestured for Jessie to get down and turned to Hawk, whose attention was still directed at the rising dust cloud.

'There's six of them, bandits,' Kinane explained.

'Well, they're comin' this way, that's for sure.'

Kinane swung around and called out to Cronkite, 'Cronk, get the horses out of sight and into the rocks. We got bandits headin' this way.'

Cronkite didn't bother to answer; he gathered up the horses with the aid of Utah and they led them out of sight.

'Hawk, help McGee finish up,' Kinane ordered the killer.

While the two men finished blotting out all sign of their presence, Kinane kept an eye on the dust cloud, and it wasn't long before he could make out the riders responsible for it.

Kinane jogged over to McGee and Hawk. 'Are you two done?'

'Barely,' Hawk explained. 'It won't stand up to close inspection.'

'Let's hope they don't look too close, then,' Kinane muttered. 'Right, up into the rocks. And don't damn well fire until I do.'

Both took their rifles and clambered up behind a large boulder. Cronkite approached Kinane and gave him his rifle.

'What do you think, Cronk?'

'I think that if they ride through here and fail to see where we've been, it'll be a damn miracle.'

Kinane nodded knowingly. 'Come on, let's take cover.'

★   ★   ★

The bandits slowed their mounts as they approached the large mass of boulders. As Jessie had signaled, there were six of them. Dirty, sweat-soaked, and unshaven, their clothes were worn and tattered, their sombreros large and drooping. Bandoleers of ammunition crisscrossed their chests. Their horses were flecked with foam and grit from hard riding.

A rider pointed at the ground adjacent to the boulder formation and the group stopped. Then he pointed at the rocks where the six were hiding.

Kinane softly cursed. They knew they were there. Without hesitation, he eased back the hammer on his Winchester.

The bandits unslung their rifles and held them at the ready.

Kinane sighted down the barrel of his weapon and started to apply pressure to the trigger.

Suddenly there was an urgent cry from the rearmost rider. The other riders turned in their saddles and looked to where he was pointing. There was a loud discussion in Spanish, and all six spurred their tired mounts brutally. The horses responded instantly and took flight, carrying their frantic riders away in a cloud of dust.

But there was no time for the ones hidden amongst the rocks to relax. Off in the direction that the bandit had pointed, another dust cloud had appeared. At its base were more riders, a lot more riders.

The situation was going from bad to worse. As the mass of horsemen rode closer, Kinane could make out the pale uniforms and peaked caps.

Rurales! About thirty of them, riding hard. The rumble of hooves slowly began to fill the air until the desert seemed to vibrate with the sound of rolling thunder.

As quickly as they'd come, they were gone. Thirty dust-caked rurales on thirty foam-flecked, hard-blowing horses.

Kinane and the others waited for the dust to clear before they emerged from the rocks. Jessie remained for a while longer just to make sure all was safe.

'That was close,' Utah Smith observed.

'Yeah,' allowed Kinane, 'too close.

McGee, get the horses, and we'll get gone before they come back.'

'So you think they'll be back?' asked Jessie.

Kinane shrugged. 'Who knows, but I sure as hell don't plan on bein' here if they do.'

The rest of the day was spent with one eye on their back trail. The afternoon sun burned in the sky, a blazing ball of fire whose heat scorched everything in the desert it touched. And finally, after the sun sank behind the distant jagged peaks, the land felt the relief of the cool night.

The small group made camp out of sight in a dry wash a short distance from the trail. They should arrive at Las Palomas the following day.

It was just after midnight when McGee shook Hawk awake to take his turn at watch. He shook him twice with no response, and was about to try again when he felt the cold barrel of Hawk's gun press hard under his chin.

'I'm awake.'

'It's your turn at watch,' McGee said as he eased the barrel of the gun to one side.

Hawk sighed loudly and sat up. He housed his Colt and stretched out his kinks from sleeping on the hard ground. 'Is it quiet?'

'Quiet enough.'

The bounty hunter watched as Hawk climbed out of his bedroll. 'What are we goin' to do about the money, Hawk?'

The killer shrugged. 'Not much we can do with them rurales back there. We'll just have to see how it all plays out.'

'If we leave it too late, that damn Mex commandant will have it all, and we'll get left with our guts full of lead.'

Hawk considered what McGee had said for a moment. 'No, I don't think he's meant to get the money.'

'What makes you so sure?'

'Well, look at it. Bell got me out of prison; hired you, the town-tamer, and another two top guns. He had the girl come along, and added to that, the money is buried a day's ride away. If the commandant was meant to get that money, we'd be takin' it right to him. If you ask me, I'd say that Kinane and the old man have somethin' up their sleeves.'

'What if you're wrong, Hawk? What then?'

'Then we wind up dead and won't have to worry any about that money.'

8

Wolf McGee rode back to the small column at a slow lope. He eased his horse to a stop, blocking the trail.

'What's up?' Kinane asked the bounty hunter, frowning.

McGee cast a thumb back over his shoulder. 'The village is about a mile or so over that ridge yonder.'

Kinane looked past him and saw the trail disappear over a low saddle-backed ridge in the distance. He looked around further and found what he was looking for. Off to the east, amongst the prickly pear and ocotillo, was a deep dry wash, gouged out by years of run-off.

'This way,' he said as he heeled his horse forward, pulling it off the trail.

The wash ran parallel with the ridge before it widened out where part of the bank had caved in, allowing the horses to climb out in the lee of a rock formation.

'We'll camp here,' Kinane announced.

'There's no water here,' Hawk pointed out.

'Hawk's right, Kinane,' Utah agreed, 'the horses need water.'

The gunfighter looked about the wash and then pointed out a small clump of shrubs. 'Dig there, you'll find all the water we need.'

Hawk snorted derisively. 'Yeah, right. In case you don't know, this is a dry wash. *Dry* being the main word.'

Kinane ignored the killer and looked at Utah. The town-tamer nodded and grabbed a shovel from the second pack horse.

'Unsaddle the horses,' Kinane ordered McGee. 'Then rub 'em down.'

Kinane then took a pair of field glasses out of his saddle bags. 'Cronk, you and Jessie come with me.'

★ ★ ★

91

Jessie passed the field glasses to Cronkite and asked Kinane, 'When do you want me to go and look around?'

'Tonight,' he replied, 'there'll be a better chance of you not bein' picked out as an American.'

She nodded. 'What is it you want me to do exactly?'

'Just have a look around. Take it all in and tell me what you see. We'll work out a final plan from that.'

'Are you sure you don't want one of us to go with her, kid?' Cronkite asked, not taking his eyes from the field glasses.

'Nope, I'll go myself.'

Jessie started to protest but Kinane cut her off. 'Cronk's right; if you have any trouble, you may need help. I'll remain outside of town while you're there. But at the first sign of trouble, get out. Clear?'

'Clear.'

★ ★ ★

The rest of the day was spent with two on watch while the others rested in the shade of the large boulders. It was hot, and the rocks were the only relief from the sun's baking rays.

As it slipped behind the mountains, a cold chill slowly filled the still air. Off to the west, a coyote could be heard as it came out to hunt for food.

Jessie was finishing preparations when Kinane and Cronkite approached.

'Are you ready?' Kinane asked.

'I think so.'

She was wearing a long cream-colored skirt, a blue cotton shirt, and a white shawl pulled tight around her shoulders. In place of her hat she wore a dark headscarf with her hair hanging long out the back.

'I think you'll pass.' Cronkite approved.

'You watch your back while I'm gone,' Kinane warned the old gunfighter. 'Don't trust anyone.'

Cronkite slapped his holstered six-gun. 'I'll have no worries, kid.'

If Kinane had any reservations, it

didn't show. Instead he turned to Jessie. 'Let's go, señorita.'

★ ★ ★

Kinane and Jessie rode their mounts back down the wash and out onto the deeply rutted main trail, using the moonlight to guide them. They followed its meandering path to the edge of town. Once there, they pulled off the trail and hid their horses in the brush.

Jessie straightened her clothes while Kinane tied the horses to a stunted poor excuse for a tree. When he finished, he took a sheathed knife from the back of his pants and held it out to the secret service agent.

'Take this,' he said quietly.

Jessie looked down; she could make out the knife in its pale leather pouch even in the dim light. 'I have my gun.'

'Take it,' he told her. 'Your gun could prove more trouble than it's worth.'

She hesitated before taking it. 'I don't know, I've only ever shot a man before.'

Kinane moved close to her and held her arms as though he would shake her violently. When he spoke next his voice had an edge to it. 'If you must use it, don't hesitate. Don't think, just do. If you think or hesitate, you're dead.'

He touched the side of her neck. 'Do it here. The blade will cut the artery and windpipe. The person will die and hopefully not make a sound. But remember, only do it if you have to.'

Jessie nodded jerkily and he let her go.

'By the way, where's your gun?'

She smiled faintly. 'Never you mind.'

★   ★   ★

Jessie slipped into Las Palomas quietly and unnoticed. She walked slowly along the edge of the darkened main street, keeping to the shadows of the adobe buildings as much as she could. Eventually it opened out into a large plaza in the center of town. At the end of the plaza was the mission garrison.

Remaining in the shadows, she watched the mission, studied it, taking in all she could. For thirty minutes she stood there, watching men come and go. All of them had the one destination or departure point: a run-down-looking cantina about halfway along the main street.

After she was finished, Jessie decided to circle the garrison itself to give her squad a fuller picture about what they were up against.

And she almost made it unseen. Almost.

As Jessie approached the stable area, a tall, thin soldier stepped from the shadows and asked, 'What are you doing here, señorita?'

Jessie froze at the man's unexpected appearance. She opened her mouth to reply but no sound came out.

'Well, I am awaiting your answer,' he demanded.

She gathered herself before speaking. 'I am enjoying such a lovely night,' she answered in Spanish, looking up at the stars.

The Mexican stepped closer. 'Alone?'

'Yes, my man is at the cantina getting drunk,' she said, hoping he wouldn't ask for a name. 'It is the third time this week.'

He took another step. 'Then maybe he is not really your man. Maybe he goes to the cantina for a little more than the tequila, yes?'

Jessie remained silent as her hand edged nervously toward the knife Kinane had given her.

Don't think, just do. His words rang in her ears. *If you think or hesitate, you're dead.*

'You need a real man, like Juan.' The soldier leered at her.

The hairs stood up on the back of Jessie's neck. Things were going from bad to worse.

Suddenly Juan lunged at her, his hands groping fiercely at her chest. The pungent odor of alcohol and stale sweat filled her nostrils. Juan's fingers closed cruelly on her right breast and the pain made Jessie gasp.

The Mexican laughed, his voice thick with lust. 'Ha, you enjoy it, yes? You like Juan?'

Instinctively, Jessie lashed out with her left hand, a stinging blow which caught him across the cheek.

Juan laughed and shrugged it off. 'You are a feisty one, señorita. I think I will enjoy your company more than I had expected.'

Once more he closed in on Jessie, and his hands pawed at her skirt as he tried to hoist it up to her waist, all the while attempting to kiss her.

The fear in Jessie rose sharply.

Don't think, just do.

Juan felt the blow to his throat, followed by a burning pain which quickly intensified. Blood spattered onto Jessie's face, warm and sticky. The Mexican staggered back, his hand clawing at the gaping wound. The look of surprise quickly changed to terror as he tried to stop the fountain of blood from the severed artery.

In a last-ditch attempt to save his life,

Juan tried to call out for help, but the moment he opened his mouth, his intended cry of alarm instead emerged as a wet gurgle. A crimson flood flowed down his chin and stained the front of his uniform.

Slowly, as the life bled out of him, Juan sank to his knees; then toppled onto his side, dead.

Jessie was horrified by what she had done. Sure, she had shot men before, but this was different. Somehow it seemed more personal.

There was no time to worry about it now. Someone could come along at any moment, and she knew the urgency of covering her deeds before anyone happened across them. After returning the bloody knife to its sheath, Jessie dragged the dead Juan out of sight into the darkened shadows beside the stable.

With that done, she walked briskly away, heading towards the edge of town and to safety.

*　*　*

Kinane sat patiently listening to the night sounds as he awaited Jessie's return. It had been a while since she'd set off into town — he'd lost track of exactly how long — but he wasn't worried yet. If she wasn't back within the next half-hour, he might think about going to look for her.

Five minutes later a noise caught his attention. Crouching behind a rock, Kinane waited, poised.

'Kinane, are you there?' came the hoarse whisper.

'Over here, Jessie,' he answered, a wave of relief sweeping over him.

'Thank God,' she said breathlessly, and stopped in front of him. 'We have to go now.'

'What happened?'

'There's no time. We need to go now,' she repeated, more urgently this time.

'OK. Mount up and let's get the hell out of here.'

9

'What happened?' Kinane asked.

Kinane, Cronkite, Jessie and Utah Smith sat around the small campfire while McGee and Hawk were on watch. Jessie told her story from the beginning as she considered the brightly dancing orange flames that licked at the air and crackled loudly.

By the time she had finished, Kinane's mind was working overtime.

'Are you alright, girl?' Cronkite asked, his voice filled with concern.

Jessie nodded. 'I think so. It's just that I've never done anything like that before.'

The old gunfighter patted her gently on the shoulder. 'It's okay, Jessie. It don't matter if you're man or woman: using a knife like that to take a life is hard to do.'

'Tell us about the garrison,' Kinane said impatiently.

'Ease up, kid,' Cronkite said, 'give her time.'

'Time is somethin' we may not have, Cronk. Especially after they find that body.'

'He's right,' Jessie agreed. 'After they find the body, who knows what they'll do?'

No one spoke, so she continued. 'On the outside it just looks like a big old mission made from adobe with fifteen-foot walls, that would be my guess. It sits at the back end of the town's main plaza. The gates are made of heavy timber and there are four towers on each corner. But that is not your biggest problem.'

'Go on,' Kinane encouraged her.

'The two towers at the front of the mission have Gatling guns in them.'

'That rules out a frontal assault,' Smith said sarcastically.

'Anythin' else?' Kinane asked, showing no concern about the information he'd just been given.

'Only the stables. But you already

know about those.'

The gunfighter thought quietly for a minute, and then asked Jessie, 'Can you get back to the stables tomorrow night without being seen?'

'I think so.'

'You'll have Cronk with you.'

'It should be no problem.'

'What do you have in mind, Kinane?' asked Smith.

'It seems to me that there is only one way into that place,' he explained, 'and that's through the front gate. So tomorrow, Hawk, McGee, you and me are goin' to ride in there.'

For the next ten minutes Kinane outlined his plan. If you could call it a plan.

Later, while Cronkite and Kinane sat having coffee, the old gunfighter voiced the doubts that were building up in his head.

'I should be goin' with you, kid,' he said.

Kinane shook his head. 'No. I need you outside.'

Cronkite looked at him doubtfully.

'Listen, if anythin' goes wrong, I want you to take Jessie and get the hell out. You're the only one I trust to do that.'

'What about you?' the old gunfighter asked.

'I'll be dead.'

*　*　*

Four riders approached the old mission with its scarred and yellowed walls the following morning, and the first thing that Kinane noticed about the plaza was the field of fire it offered the Gatling guns.

'Damn street feeds in like a funnel,' Hawk observed.

'Them guns turn it into a killin' field,' Utah said.

'Kinane, the wall,' said Hawk, drawing the gunfighter's attention.

They all looked in the direction of the killer's gaze. There was a small area of pockmarked wall with craters gouged

104

out of it. Intermingled amongst the damage was the brown rust-stained color of dried blood.

'No prizes for guessin' what goes on there,' Utah stated.

The four drew their horses up to the big, reinforced, dark timber gates. A small door, situated five feet above the hard-packed earth, opened, and a man's unshaven, nut-brown face filled the void.

'What do you want, gringos?' he asked, not bothering to conceal his contempt for the men from north of the border.

'We want to see your commandant,' Kinane said, ignoring the man's open hostility.

The soldier looked the strangers over and growled, 'My commandant is busy, go away.'

'Your commandant will see us,' Kinane persisted.

The guard snorted derisively. 'Go away before I have you shot down like dogs.'

'Tell him it's about his American prisoners. Tell him we are here with his money.'

The Mexican's eyes showed a hint of uncertainty as he digested what the gringo had told him. He abruptly slammed the small door.

Kinane thought that right about now the guard would be running across the parade ground.

'This is a damn bad idea, Kinane,' Hawk complained once more. 'As soon as he finds out we don't have the money with us, there is a fair chance that Mex son of a bitch in there will shoot us.'

'It's possible,' Kinane agreed.

Before any more opinions could be aired there was a sound of wood scraping from the other side of the wall, followed by the screeching complaint of stiff hinges as the right-side gate swung open to let them in.

'I guess we're about to find out,' Kinane mumbled.

The four kneed their horses forward,

and once inside the mission walls the gate swung closed, trapping them inside. There was immediate activity as armed rurales spilled out. All stood with their weapons ready as they lined up on each side of the parade ground.

The Americans halted their mounts and sat with both hands on their saddle pommels, well away from their six-guns. A man high on a parapet shouted an order, and every rurale who held a rifle snapped it up into line.

'This is goin' well.' Hawk's voice dripped with sarcasm.

'Shut up, Hawk,' Kinane snapped, 'and don't do anythin' stupid.'

'Too late, I followed you in here.'

The four waited for a brief time under the quickly warming sun before Mendoza appeared. He was a solid-built man, but by no means big. He stood proud and erect, his face was clean-shaven, and his dark eyes were set wide apart. There was an air of arrogance that radiated about him. His gaudy uniform was freshly pressed and his chest was puffed out like a strutting peacock.

Mendoza put on his best smile, spread his arms wide and greeted them loudly, 'Gentlemen, welcome to you all. Please step down from your horses.'

Slowly, the four did as they were asked, and the commandant continued, 'I am told you are here about the senator and his family.'

'That's right,' Kinane confirmed.

Mendoza's face fell and took on a sullen expression. 'I am sorry to tell you, but the senator died suddenly last night. His heart, I think, very sad.'

'What about his wife?' Kinane asked, his face passive.

The commandant shrugged his shoulders. 'Alas, she has died too. Very sad that they both should die in the one night.'

'You mean you killed 'em,' sneered Hawk.

'Shut it, Hawk,' Kinane snapped hurriedly.

A dark cloud flitted across Mendoza's face, then quickly disappeared.

'What about his daughter?' Hawk asked ignoring Kinane.

'She is fine, I think.'

'You think.' Kinane raised his eyebrows.

The commandant shrugged nonchalantly. 'When she was told about her parents she was distressed. But that was to be expected. I have not seen her since then.'

'Maybe we best take her now, then, before she too happens to die in your custody.'

Mendoza nodded. 'Yes, it probably would be best. Do you have the money, señor?'

'The amount we have, Commandant, was for three people. But only one remains alive. It would seem a price adjustment should be in order.'

'No,' Mendoza snapped, 'the price is still the same.'

'But two of them are dead.'

'Yes, they are,' the commandant said through gritted teeth. His face darkened with rage at the gringo's open defiance. 'And so can one more be, along with the rest of you.'

'Ease up, Kinane,' Hawk cautioned.

But the gunfighter's voice grew cold as he said, 'Do you think your men can kill me before I put a bullet in your head, Commandant?'

A look of uncertainty crept into Mendoza's face. 'What good is it if we are all dead, gringo?'

'Fair point.'

The relief was evident on the Mexican's face. 'Good, then we are agreed. The price is still the same. Now, where is the money?'

'It's buried in the desert,' Kinane answered.

'You do not have it?'

'No.'

A tremor ran through the commandant as his anger once more threatened to explode, and his words came out with a caustic edge to them. 'I warn you, gringo, I do not play games.'

'We take the girl, and you bring a couple of men with you when we take you to the money.'

Mendoza shook his head. 'No, I don't think so.'

'It's the only way it's goin' to happen.'

Mendoza whispered something to a man who stood close to him, who then ran across to a small building that stood against the east wall.

Moments later he emerged, dragging a struggling Alice Sugden with him. She was filthy, scared, her dress torn, but she still had some fight left in her. That was good.

The rurale half-carried, half-dragged Alice across the parade ground, and stopped when he reached his commandant's side. Mendoza pulled his pistol and placed the cold steel barrel against the side of the woman's head, bringing her struggles to an immediate stop.

'Now, we shall try again. Drop your guns.'

None of the four moved.

Mendoza cocked the six-gun, and the dry triple click sounded thunderous in the sudden silence. 'Drop your guns.'

'Okay, drop 'em,' Kinane said resignedly.

'You know what happens if we do,' Hawk said, openly challenging the decision.

'It's nothin' we didn't expect,' Kinane acknowledged.

McGee unbuckled his gun-belt, followed by Utah Smith, then Hawk, and finally Kinane. They let their weapons fall into the dirt of the parade ground.

As a rurale picked up the discarded belts, Hawk said softly, 'Just so you know, I'll be gettin' them back.'

Mendoza lowered the six-gun and eased down the hammer. He then ordered the rurale to take Alice back to her cell.

'Now, gringos — ' The arrogance was back in the commandant's voice. ' — this is what is going to happen. No more games. One of you will be given the chance to live. The others will be shot in the plaza.'

Kinane remembered the stained,

pockmarked area on the wall they'd seen as they rode up to the gate.

Mendoza continued, 'All that man has to do is tell me where the money is.'

The four remained silent.

'Remember, the first one to tell will live,' Mendoza encouraged.

Still there was silence.

The commandant drew his six-gun once more and walked towards the small group of prisoners. He stopped short of them before he moved to the left and halted in front of Wolf McGee. Then he raised his gun.

Every man knew what would happen next. The gun stopped level with the bounty hunter's forehead.

McGee swallowed hard and a film of sweat broke out on his face, his fear immediately evident. Once again, the hammer of the pistol being drawn back sounded unbelievably loud.

Mendoza looked into McGee's eyes and smiled. A cold, cruel smile. Then he started to apply pressure to the gun's trigger.

It was all too much for the bounty hunter. 'Wait! I'll tell you where it is; I'll show you, even.'

'Damn you, McGee,' Hawk cursed.

Kinane and Utah remained silent.

'Do we have a deal?' McGee went on hurriedly. 'I show you and you let me live. Let me go.'

Mendoza let the hammer down and lowered his gun. 'That is what I said.'

The relief on the bounty hunter's face was evident. But then, with a dismissive wave of his hand, the commandant ordered, 'Lock them up.'

Rurales ran forward and started pushing the four towards the cells.

'Wait!' cried McGee once more. 'We had a deal.'

'And so we do, my gringo friend. I will send someone for you directly.'

Mendoza turned to his captain, Raoul. 'I want forty men with horses saddled and ready to ride by noon.'

'Yes, Commandant,' the captain answered, showing no concern about being left with so few himself. 'But what if there is no money?'

'Then I will kill them all.'

The captain nodded, and went to walk away when Mendoza stopped him.

'That other issue, Raoul — the dead man. Did you look into it?'

'*Si*, the man was well-known for chasing the señoritas.' He paused, then added, 'And the señoras. It would not surprise me if it was a jealous husband who killed him, Commandant.'

'Fine. I will deal with it when I return.'

'*Si*, Commandant.'

10

'Damn yeller son of a bitch!' Hawk's voice echoed throughout the block built hallway.

They had been put into separate cells. Kinane had suspected that this would occur, and that was why he'd ensured they still had backup on the outside. With Mendoza taking three-quarters of his force out into the desert on a forlorn quest, he could not have hoped for better. And that was why his plan changed.

* * *

'Somethin's happenin',' Cronkite observed as he passed the field glasses to Jessie.

She put them up to her eyes and watched as the double-line column of rurales rode from Las Palomas, kicking

116

up a large, pale dust cloud. Jessie let the glasses settle on the gaudily dressed rider at the front of the column.

'I don't understand,' Jessie said, confused. 'Mendoza is riding out and taking all his men with him.'

'No, I don't think our Mexican friend would be that stupid,' Cronkite said doubtfully. 'I'd say he's left some behind; but, judging by the size of his force, not many.'

'Here.' Jessie passed the glasses back to the old gunfighter. 'Two back behind the lead rider.'

Cronkite found Mendoza at the head of the column, and then let his gaze drift back until he found what he was looking for amidst the rising dust.

'I'll be damned.'

'It is him, isn't it?' she asked.

'It's McGee alright,' he confirmed.

'But what's he up to?'

'The son of a bitch is takin' them to the money. My guess is he's tryin' to save his own skin. Somethin' must have gone wrong.'

'What do you think will happen when he finds out there is none?'

'I expect the commandant will get madder than a wet hen and shoot him on the spot. After that, he'll go thunderin' back and do the same to the others,' Cronkite surmised, 'if they're still alive.'

'Do you think they know about us?'

'I guess we'll find out,' Cronkite said as he passed the glasses back. 'Here, take these. I'll get the horses ready just in case. Keep an eye out. If they leave the trail, come runnin' and we'll head out into the desert.'

But the rurale column didn't stop, leave the trail, or even glance sideways. They kept their eyes straight ahead and left a pall of dust in their wake.

Jessie breathed a heavy sigh of relief and scrambled back down from her hiding position to find Cronkite. The old gunfighter was waiting with the saddled horses.

'It's all clear,' she told him. 'They kept on going.'

'That's somethin', at least.'

'What do we do now?'

'We stick to the plan.'

'But what if he's already killed them?' Jessie inquired.

'Then we won't be any use to 'em, will we?' Cronkite said bluntly.

*   *   *

'They've gone,' Utah Smith said loudly as he stepped back from the small window, blocked up with iron bars covered in a rusty scale.

'Yeah,' confirmed Hawk, 'with that damn yeller McGee ridin' right up front with 'em.'

'It won't do him any good,' Kinane assured them.

'What was that you said?' asked Hawk.

Kinane raised his voice to another level. 'I said, it won't do him any good.'

'Why not?' asked Smith.

'Yeah, why not?' echoed Hawk.

'Because there is no money.'

'What?' Hawk again.

'Are you deaf or somethin'?' Utah snapped. 'He said there's no damn money.'

'I blamed well heard that part,' the killer called back. 'What I want to know is, why?'

'I'd like to know the answer to that question too, Kinane,' the town-tamer allowed.

'The government put us together because they thought we stood a good chance of pulling off a rescue without paying money. They also thought that if Mendoza got his hands on the money, he would kill us all.'

'That's why you buried the chest a day's ride from here,' stated Hawk.

'Yes; if we were goin' to get out of here, we needed time. And him ridin' off after the money gives us that. I just didn't think he would take most of the garrison to go after it. That works better for us. We may even get out of here alive.'

'You might have let us in on the plan.'

'Didn't know who I could trust,' Kinane

said truthfully, 'and as it happens, I was right.'

'So, what now?' asked Utah.

'We wait for dark.'

★ ★ ★

Out in the desert the sounds of the night came alive and a chill settled into the air. A coyote yipped, and then a cougar's human-like scream stretched out across the land and caused the horses to twitch nervously.

'Whoa, horse,' Cronkite soothed the animal, 'he's just lost. He won't bother us none.'

'What was that?' Jessie asked, never having heard a cougar before.

'It was only a cougar, nothin' to worry about,' the old gunfighter dismissed the question.

'Was it close?'

Cronkite shook his head. 'No, he's out there in the desert a far piece. Normally they stay up in the mountains.'

Jessie was noticeably nervous as she looked about trying to pierce the darkness with her gaze. The sun had been down for an hour and soon the moon would be up, casting its dull silvery light across the desert landscape, turning rocks and shrubs into inanimate sentinels of the night.

'What will we do with the pack horses?' Jessie asked, concerned. 'We can't leave them here.'

'We'll take 'em in closer to town and leave them with our own mounts. They should be alright there for a while. Are you ready to go?'

'Yes, I think so.'

'Let's go, then.'

A time later, as the moon started its climb into a night sky alive with millions of glittering stars, they hitched their horses to a bush outside of Las Palomas.

'If everythin' goes right, I'll come back and get them after,' Cronkite said.

Once more Jessie made her way through the shadows that lined the main street, with the old gunfighter following behind. She moved into a narrow, dark alley beside an adobe building, and the mission loomed up in front of them.

'Where are the stables?' asked Cronkite.

'Around to the left.'

'Wait here,' he told her.

The old gunfighter slipped away silently and disappeared down the alley. He circled wide and came up to the stables. He watched from the darkness, waiting until he was certain there was only one guard.

He was about to move when he was startled by a soft footfall behind him. He whirled, six-gun leaping into his hand. It levelled with its hammer on full cock.

Jessie gasped as she jumped back, startled by the swiftness of the old gunfighter.

'Damn it, girl,' Cronkite whispered harshly, 'I told you to stay put. Damn well almost got yourself shot.'

'I'm sorry, I thought you might need help.'

The old gunfighter eased the hammer down on his Colt and holstered it as he shook his head. He sighed and said firmly, 'Wait here. I'll be back in a minute.'

Jessie nodded. 'Okay.'

'I mean it, girl. Don't move.'

Before Jessie could respond, he was gone.

*　　*　　*

The guard was sloppy and lazy. This surprised Cronkite because he was sure the garrison was aware of the dead man from the previous night. But this rurale spent most of his time with his back turned to the outside world, and was none the wiser about his imminent demise.

Once aware of his impending doom, it was too late. Cronkite's rough, calloused hand clamped firmly over his mouth, and the knife in his opposite hand had been driven up between two of the man's lower ribs and into his heart. The guard died without making a solitary sound.

Cronkite lowered the Mexican to the ground and wiped the bloody knife on the guard's uniform. He then dragged him inside the dully lit stables where he hid the body in an empty stall.

Jessie watched it all unfold from where she was hidden, and as she remembered the night before, a cold chill made her shiver. Then Cronkite was back beside her.

'Come with me,' he whispered. 'I need you to keep watch while I saddle the horses.'

Following the old gunfighter closely, she crossed to the stables.

'Wait here in the doorway and keep an eye out.'

'What if somebody comes?'

'You've still got the knife Kinane gave you — use it.'

★　★　★

It's time, Kinane thought as he swung his legs to the floor and sat on the edge of what passed for a bed. The guard came and checked on them every hour religiously. This time he would be ready. With one of the oldest tricks in the book.

When the guard came to check, he found Kinane's cell empty. At least, that was what he thought. In truth, Kinane was hidden out of sight, and the small window in the cell door gave the Mexican only a very limited field of vision, so he had no option other than to open the door to check.

'¡*Madre de Dios!*' the rurale gasped as his fear of his commandant's brutality overrode any concept of caution. The key rattled furiously in the lock as the guard tried desperately to get the door open. He felt relief as the key turned and the door swung open. He rushed in quickly, then realized his mistake. All too late.

Kinane grasped the off-balance guard by his collar and ran him straight at the far wall, his head connecting with an immoveable object with a resounding wet smack. The guard slumped lifeless on the floor of the stinking, cockroach-ridden cell.

Kinane bent down and relieved the guard of his pistol. He checked its loads. He found a handful of cartridges in the dead man's pocket and stuffed them into his own, then crossed to the door where the keys hung waiting in the lock.

The first cell he came to was Hawk's. The gunfighter looked surprised before he grumbled, 'About damn time, Kinane.'

'You're welcome,' the gunfighter said.

Next, he opened Utah's cell, and the three stood in the hallway.

'Where do they have the girl?' Hawk asked, looking about.

'Leave her where she is,' Kinane ordered.

Both men stared at the gunfighter, confused. 'Why?' they asked together.

'We're not leavin',' Kinane explained.

'Oh hell,' muttered Utah Smith.

Hawk's jaw dropped. 'You're crazy, right? For a minute, there I thought you said we were stayin'.'

Kinane nodded. 'That's right.'

There was a heavy silence before Kinane continued, 'We are goin' to take this place, and when that son of a bitch Mendoza comes back tomorrow, he's goin' to get the surprise of his life.'

'Do you know how many men are left here?' Hawk asked, bewildered.

'I know that there's one less.'

The killer shook his head. 'You're a damned crazy fool.'

'He's right, Hawk,' Utah added. 'We need to try and stop Mendoza here. He rode out with forty men. I counted 'em when I was lookin' out the window.'

'So, by rights,' Kinane said, doing a quick calculation, 'there should be nine left without the man in my cell.'

'Even if we do manage to take this place,' Hawk protested, 'what hope do we happy few have against forty rurales?'

'Maybe none,' Kinane allowed.

'We'll have them Gatlin' guns,' Utah put in, 'they'll damn well whittle 'em down some.'

'Okay,' declared Hawk, 'let's do it.'

11

Outside the cell block, the parade ground was dappled in natural and artificial light. Kinane, Hawk and Utah slipped out through a crack in the jail door and around the corner of the building into a dark shadow.

'You two take care of the guard towers,' Kinane whispered. 'But do it quietly.'

'What are you goin' to be doin'?' asked Hawk.

'I'll let Cronk and Jessie in, then I'll go after that feller Mendoza left in charge. That will leave the barracks.'

'That Mendoza must be stupid,' surmised Hawk. 'He didn't even leave enough men to rotate the watches properly.'

'All he was thinkin' about when he rode out of here was the money,' Kinane explained. 'Let's go.'

Utah and Hawk disposed of the guards quietly and efficiently. It wasn't hard. The four soldiers were tired and, like their comrade whom Cronkite had encountered at the stables, weren't paying much attention.

After the two guards at the front of the mission were neutralized, Kinane let himself out through the main gate and circled around to the stables. He emitted a low whistle which was answered by Cronkite. The old gunfighter emerged from the shadows holding a cocked six-gun. He was closely followed by Jessie, who had her Remington out and ready to fire.

'Damn good to see you, kid.' Cronkite smiled and holstered his gun. 'The girl here was startin' to worry about you. Kept wonderin' if you were alive or not. Of course, I told her there was nothin' to worry about.'

'Yeah, well, it weren't that straightforward,' Kinane muttered, confirming what they had suspected.

'Uh-huh. We saw 'em ride out of here with McGee.'

'Turned yeller at the first sign of things gettin' tough.'

'Well, the horses are ready,' the old gunfighter told him. 'You just get the others and that senator feller, and we'll be gone.'

'We're not leavin', Cronk.'

'Say what?'

'We're stayin',' Kinane stated with finality. 'The senator and his wife are both dead.'

'Oh no,' Jessie gasped.

'Their daughter is still alive in a cell,' Kinane continued, 'but we're stayin'. Mendoza took most of his men with him. Once we have control of this place, we'll wait for him to return and we'll turn his damned Gatlin' guns loose on him. He needs to be stopped, Cronk.'

Cronkite nodded. 'Alright, kid, I'm in.'

'Jessie, what about you?' Kinane asked.

'I'll stay,' she confirmed.

'Right. As far as I know, there should be three guards in the barracks. When Mendoza left, he just about cleaned this place out. Can you and Jessie take care of it?'

'Sure.' The old gunfighter nodded positively.

'Good. You'll find me at the Commandant's office.'

*   *   *

The office was lit by the low glow of a dull lamp. Kinane could peer in through a small gap in the curtained window. The rurale who had been left in charge was seated behind a large desk, smoking a cigar.

Kinane moved from the window to the whitewashed door and cocked the unfamiliar pistol in his hand. He drew in a deep breath and kicked open the door, splintering the latch.

The effect of the door crashing back had the desired effect and Raoul froze in place, cigar halfway to his gaping mouth. The terrified captain's first thought was about Mendoza, but when he saw Kinane filling the doorway with a handful of gun, it quickly disappeared.

'Just hold it right there.' Kinane's voice held a menacing tone, and the gunfighter moved further into the room.

'How . . . how did you get out?' The rurale stumbled over the question.

'I think you should concern yourself more with what happens next.'

'You will not escape,' Raoul said, starting to regain his composure. 'My men will stop you.'

'Right about now, Mex, you are the only one of your men left,' Kinane told him coldly.

Raoul turned pale in the dull light, 'It is not possible.'

'It is.'

'*Madre de Dios*, the commandant is going to put me against the wall and have me shot,' he said in abject terror.

Kinane couldn't have cared less. 'Not my problem.'

'Are you alright in there, kid?' a familiar voice called from outside.

'Sure, Cronk, come on in.'

Jessie and the old gunfighter entered the office. 'Everythin' looks to be under control,' Cronkite asserted. 'Them fellers we found in the barracks are trussed up and sleepin' like babies.'

'Here's another one for you to tie up,' Kinane said, waving the six-gun in his direction. Then he asked, 'Where's all our weapons, Mex?'

'In the armory,' Raoul mumbled despondently.

Cronkite finished tying the man up, and Kinane motioned for Jessie and his friend to follow him outside, where he found Utah and Hawk.

'Have any problems?' he asked them.

'Not a one,' answered Utah.

'Good. There's a feller in there,' Kinane pointed at the door to the office, 'and some more in the barracks. Find the key to the armory, get our guns and such, then lock 'em up in the cells.'

Kinane turned to Jessie. 'Can you get Alice Sugden and bring her here to the commandant's office?'

'Sure.'

'See that's she's okay, then come and find me. There's somethin' I need you to do.'

'What is it we're goin' to be doin', kid?' asked Cronkite.

When Kinane told him what he wanted, the old gunfighter frowned. 'It might work.'

'Let's hope it does,' Kinane said stoically.

★ ★ ★

'Dig faster, gringo, or I shall bury you in the hole when you have finished,' Mendoza urged McGee, who was digging by firelight.

'I could use some help, Commandant,' he complained.

'Just shut up and dig. Find me my

money,' the Mexican hissed.

It felt to McGee like he'd been digging forever. His muscles ached from exertion, and although it was a cool night, a thin film of perspiration covered his exposed skin. Then the shovel he was using hit something with a muffled thud.

The bounty hunter smiled with relief and looked up at Mendoza. 'I found it.'

'You two,' Mendoza snapped at a couple of men standing closest to the gaping hole, 'help him get it out. Quickly!'

Another five minutes passed before the chest was heaved from its desert bed and dumped onto the ground beside the hole.

'Get it open!' the commandant shouted impatiently.

A rurale shot the lock off, and lifted the lid so that it swung back over and rested on the sand.

Every man around the chest froze — except for Mendoza, whose body began to tremble as his rage built to a dangerous level.

McGee paled. 'Aw hell, Commandant, I didn't know it was empty. Kinane never said. Shoot, we never even looked in there before.'

'It would seem, gringo,' Mendoza said in a deep voice filled with venom, 'that we have both been double-crossed.'

'Damn straight! That son of a bitch double-crossed us both,' the bounty hunter reiterated as he tried to grasp at something that would save his life.

'I assure you, gringo, that he will pay a high price for his deception,' the commandant told McGee. 'But, alas, you will not be there to see it.'

'But I didn't know, Commandant,' the bounty hunter pleaded. 'I told you we never saw in the box. Do you think I would drag you all the way out here knowing that the chest was empty?'

Mendoza shook his head. 'No, I do not think you would have; but I do know one thing.'

McGee looked at him quizzically. 'What's that?'

'It will not be empty for much longer,' Mendoza snarled viciously, and drew his sidearm. He thumbed back the hammer as it came into line with McGee's forehead and squeezed the trigger.

The thunder of the gunshot filled the still desert night, and the bounty hunter's head snapped back. As the bullet exploded out the back of it, a fine spray of blood spattered the face of the rurale nearest to McGee, causing him to blanch involuntarily.

'Get to your horses!' Mendoza shouted. 'You two, bury him in that empty box.'

* * *

When Jessie found Kinane, he had just finished bringing the horses inside the walls with the help of Cronkite.

'How's the girl?' he asked.

She shrugged. 'Hard to tell.'

'Do you think she's up to a horse ride?'

'Tonight?'

'Yeah, tonight,' Kinane confirmed.

Jessie was confused. 'I guess so. But I thought we were staying?'

'We are, but you and Alice are leavin' tonight,' he explained.

'The hell I am,' she said defiantly.

Cronkite tried hard not to smile. 'I'm stayin' here with you. You'll need all the guns you can get when Mendoza returns.'

'You're right,' Kinane acknowledged. 'But you're still not stayin', Jessie. We need to get Alice Sugden back, and I promised your boss I'd return you safe as well.'

'It's not for you to say. So, I'm staying,' she said, her jaw set firm.

'Damn you, woman. Just do like I say. You ain't stayin', and that's it. Don't make me tie you to the saddle. Now, go and get the girl ready.'

Without another word, Jessie stormed off.

'What the hell are you smilin' about, old man?' Kinane snapped as he turned his anger on Cronkite.

'Well, kid, I was just figurin' that if we get out of this alive, you two will make a mighty fine couple.'

'Oh, shut up!'

And with that Kinane was gone.

'Yes, siree.' Cronkite laughed almost childishly. 'A mighty fine couple.'

★ ★ ★

'Are you ready to go?' Kinane asked cautiously.

'Yes,' was the single-word reply.

'You've got extra ammunition just in case?'

Without turning from adjusting her saddle girth strap, Jessie said, 'Yes.'

Alice Sugden sat patiently on a sorrel horse from the rurale stables, Kinane turned to her. 'Miss Alice, you listen to Jessie. Do whatever she tells you to do and you'll be fine.'

The young lady just nodded.

Kinane turned back to face the other woman, who was now finished and preparing to mount. 'Jessie.'

She halted and turned around.

'Follow the trail until just before dawn, then find a place to hole up. Once Mendoza and his men have passed, you should have an easy run to the border. We'll catch up to you if we can.'

For a short while there was a heavy silence, and then Jessie did something totally unexpected. Taking Kinane by surprise, she kissed him hard and passionately. When she broke away, she stood waiting for his reaction, but Kinane was too stunned to speak.

His mind raced. He tried to speak, but no sound emanated.

Suddenly Jessie's frustration resurfaced. 'Damn you, Kinane!'

She mounted her horse and vented her fury once more. 'Go and get yourself killed. See if I care.'

With that, they were gone, out through the gates and beyond.

Cronkite walked over and slapped Kinane on the back with a little more force than necessary. 'That there girl really likes you, kid.'

'Oh, shut up before I shoot you.'

The old gunfighter guffawed, then once more his expression grew serious. 'You know, kid, I been thinkin', and we could really use some help.'

'Tell me somethin' I don't know,' Kinane snapped testily.

'Just listen for a moment before you go gettin' all hot and bite my head off.'

'Sorry, Cronk,' Kinane apologized to his friend. 'Keep goin'.'

'Well, it seems to me we got all the help we need right outside these walls.'

'You mean the villagers?'

'Yep. If we can get them to help, we'll have a fightin' chance of gettin' out of here in one piece. And it'll be a lot better plan than the one we already have.'

Kinane nodded. 'That's all well and good, but how are we goin' to do that?'

'You just leave the particulars to me. I'll work on it,' Cronkite said confidently.

Kinane watched as his friend headed toward the gates.

His next port of call was the armory, where he found Hawk and Utah still loading rifles. 'How's it goin'?'

'Still a few to do, but we're almost done,' the town-tamer answered.

'Good. When you're finished, space them out along the parapets. Once it all kicks off, we ain't goin' to have a whole lot of time to reload them. Did you find extra magazines for the Gatlin's?'

'Yeah,' said Hawk, 'all we got to do is stack 'em next to the guns.'

'We also found some barrels of gunpowder,' Utah informed him.

'Any fuse?'

'Yeah, a whole roll.'

Kinane half-smiled. 'Seems to me things are startin' to look up.'

'How do you figure that?' Hawk inquired.

'Wait here,' Kinane ordered and then hurried off, leaving the two confused men behind him.

Kinane found what he was looking

for in the commandant's quarters. Two wool blankets and one of Mendoza's bed sheets.

When he walked back into the armory with his load, Hawk asked, 'What the hell are you doin' with all that?'

Kinane smiled in the dim light. 'I want you to find any small bits of metal you can lay your hands on. Nails, lead shot, whatever. It doesn't matter. We are goin' to make ourselves some equalizers.'

'Some what?' asked Hawk.

'Some bombs.'

★   ★   ★

Just before dawn, some miles to the north, Jessie and Alice Sugden guided their weary horses off the main trail and into a deep gully, scoured out over time and lined with mesquite. They followed it for a distance before they dismounted.

'We'll leave the saddles on the horses,

and give them some water from the spare canteens,' Jessie told Alice.

'Do you think we'll make it back?' the senator's daughter asked.

'Sure we will,' Jessie said, sounding as confident as possible. 'After the rurales pass, we'll keep riding for the river.'

The sun was starting to lift its head over a distant ridge, long fingers of orange light reaching out across the sky, when the women heard the low rumbling of horses' hooves.

'What's that noise?' Alice asked, uncertain.

'Horses,' answered Jessie. 'Lots of them. Wait here and don't move.'

Jessie scrambled back along the wash and climbed to its lip. She lifted her head and peered over, still hidden by the mesquite.

It was light enough, and she was close enough, to make out Mendoza at the head of the column of rurales — and to see that McGee was no longer with them.

The column rode past in a low

cacophony of rumbling hooves and snorting beasts. Dust kicked up in the still morning air hung like an eerie fog, the riders on their steeds wraiths of a bygone age. And then they were gone, with just the dust to tell of their passing.

Jessie heaved a heavy sigh of relief and hurried back to where she had left Alice and the horses.

She was gone.

* * *

Kinane and the others were finishing their preparations for the return of Mendoza. Kinane hoped Cronkite could muster up some help. Four well-placed shots could finish it all for them, and at this point he didn't feel like dying.

Still wrapped up in his own thoughts, Kinane didn't see his friend approach with a small, shabbily dressed Mexican at his side. 'I've found us some help, kid.'

Kinane looked up and swapped his

glance from the Mexican to his friend and then back again before saying, 'One man, is that it?'

He looked sadly at the small man. 'Thank you, señor, but I'm afraid you would die for no reason. Go back home to your family.'

'Hold up, kid,' Cronkite protested. 'It's not what you think. This feller here is what passes in town for a mayor. His name is Romero, and he assures me that he is able to get more villagers to help out.'

Kinane looked at the man and asked, 'Are you sure you want to get involved?'

Romero nodded. '*Si*, señor.'

'You know there's a good chance you could all get killed?'

'*Si* señor, but the Commandant has had us living like cowardly dogs for too long now. Now is the time to fight back.'

'How many men can you scrape together?'

Romero shrugged. 'Ten, maybe twelve.'

'Will they be willing to risk it all and

stand with gringos?'

'I am sure of it.'

Kinane nodded. 'Get 'em together.'

As he watched him go, he murmured, 'Hell, Cronk, I hope they all don't get killed for nothin'.'

★ ★ ★

Looking at the horse tracks, Jessie surmised that Alice Sugden had gotten scared and ridden straight out into the desert, away from the trail and the threat of Mendoza's riders.

The government agent had been following the tracks for around an hour as they wound their way through country dotted with prickly pear and ocotillo. The landscape was harsh and only fit for those adapted to live there. Now, with the sun higher in the sky, the temperature was steadily climbing, and Alice had no water.

'Damn that girl,' Jessie cursed aloud.

She couldn't believe that Alice had been stupid enough to run off out into desert country on her own. Yes, she was scared, but to do something like this was signing her own death warrant. She might as well have stayed locked up where she was.

Thirty minutes later, things went from bad to worse. Three riders had cut across Alice's tracks and, after stopping for a brief time, fallen in behind the fleeing girl and followed her trail.

Jessie checked her weapons. It looked as though the senator's daughter would need rescuing again.

* * *

When Romero returned, he had eleven men with him. All of them were dressed in a similar shabby fashion to the small Mexican. Kinane called them all together and outlined the plan. He squatted down and scratched out a diagram in the dust of the parade ground.

Kinane looked up at Cronkite. 'I want you and Utah mannin' the Gatlin' guns, with Romero and three of his men up on the walls as well.' He shifted his gaze to Romero. 'I take it your men can shoot?'

The small Mexican nodded.

'Where does that leave us?' Hawk asked.

'You are with me on the outside,' Kinane answered seriously.

'We're what?' the killer asked incredulously.

'Me, you, and the leftover villagers are goin' to be hidin' in the buildin's along the main street. Once them Gatlin' guns open up, we'll wait for the rurales to turn tail. Then we'll hit them with our little gunpowder surprises.'

'Then what?'

'Then we fight like hell until we're dead or all of them are.'

Hawk spat a globule of saliva into the dirt. 'Just what I like. A simple plan.'

12

By mid-morning, Jessie was closing the gap on those in front of her. The trail indicated that the pursuers had caught up with Alice Sugden, and after a brief struggle, all four horses had continued east.

The trail lead through rugged terrain dotted with rock and sandstone formations before it dipped down into a steep-sided wash where it snaked along, guided by its walls.

Suddenly a scream electrified the air, closely followed by loud, pleading protests. Instead of spurring her horse forward, Jessie hurriedly dismounted and took the Winchester from the saddle boot. Leaving her horse ground-hitched, she eased along the steeper left side of the wash, because that was the way it turned further on.

When Jessie reached the corner, she

crouched behind a large rock which had been gouged from the bank by years of wildly rushing water. She eased her way around it and peered beyond. There, surrounded by three Mexican bandits, was Alice Sugden, her dress partially torn away at the shoulder, exposing milky white skin.

The three Mexicans smiled evilly. They were like three wolves about to devour long-awaited, mouth-watering prey. They pushed Alice from man to man, and each time another tear opened in her clothing. All the while she begged them to stop.

As quietly as possible, Jessie eared back the hammer of her Winchester. She came out from behind the rock with the rifle levelled.

'Hold it right there and get your hands up,' she snapped.

The three bandits froze.

'I said, get your hands up.' Her voice cut through the air like the snap of a bullwhip.

The men's hands slowly elevated.

'Thank God you're here,' Alice gasped. 'These heathens were about ... about to ... ' Her voice trailed away.

'Shut up!' Jessie snarled. 'I'll deal with you later.'

By now all the bandits were facing her, their arms still raised. The three men were dressed in what most people would class as rags. And from the odor carried on the breeze drifting towards her, Jessie guessed they were old rags. She wrinkled her nose in disgust at the smelly, unwashed, unshaven animals in front of her.

'It would seem that this is our lucky day, amigos,' one of the bandits said loudly. 'Now we have two gringo women to entertain us.'

'Shut your damn mouth, you disgusting pig,' Jessie barked.

'She is a feisty one.' The same man smiled cruelly. 'She will give us much pleasure.'

Jessie ignored the comment. 'Alice, get your horse and run theirs off.'

The same Mexican stepped forward. 'They will not go far. We will have them back in no time.'

'Alice, wait,' Jessie changed her mind; after all, the man was probably right. 'Bring their horses with us.'

The man's face remained passive. 'You will not leave us here without our horses, señorita.'

'Damn right I will,' she snorted. 'I want your guns too.'

He shook his head. 'No, señorita, you will not take our weapons. To leave us here without horses or guns is to leave us to die.'

'Just be thankful I'm leaving you with a little water,' Jessie said coldly.

The bandit's face turned into a mask of hatred. He started to tremble as his rage built. 'Ernesto, Pablo.'

The remaining two bandits eased out from their compadre's side.

'I told you to drop your guns, now do it.'

'No, señorita, I'm afraid you will have to take them.'

A calmness washed over Jessie. An acceptance of the inevitable. The bandit's confidence that the woman would not fire was high. He smiled: a big, disarming smile. And went for his gun.

Yes, Jessie might be a woman; but damn, she could shoot.

Her rifle belched flame, and her first bullet took the Mexican in his chest, knocking him from his feet. The echo of that first shot rang out across the desert.

Jessie quickly worked the lever as she swung the Winchester into line with the bandit called Pablo. He stood shocked at the violent death dealt to his friend by this seemingly helpless gringo woman.

Once more the Winchester barked, and a hollow slap reverberated about the wash as the .44 caliber slug hit Pablo in the middle and exploded out his back in a spray of crimson.

The third bandit, Ernesto, had his own gun out and fired. A shot scorched the skin of Jessie's left arm as it passed through the material of her shirt. The shock caused her to lose her grip on the rifle, and it clattered to the ground.

With nerve endings screaming at her to move, Jessie did just that. Drawing her Remington, she bent low and scampered right, firing as she went.

The bandit fired more shots at her. All came close but none found their mark. Jessie fired two shots of her own. The first flew wild, but the second found the fleshy part of Ernesto's right thigh.

He screamed as his leg crumpled beneath him, unable to support his weight. Trying to remain balanced, the Mexican fought to bring his six-gun into line.

Jessie fired her Remington twice more. The first and second bullets hit Ernesto in the chest a finger's breadth apart. Without any sound, the bandit toppled sideways into the dirt, dead before his head touched the dry wash floor.

Covering the prone forms with her Remington, Jessie walked over to them, ready for anything. Evidently there was no need for her to be on edge. Two were dead, one was dying. She stood looking down at the mortally wounded man. He looked at her through pain-filled eyes. His life-giving blood steadily drained, feeding the parched desert sands.

The bandit opened his mouth to speak, but all that came from his mouth was a wet gurgle, followed by a cough and a long sigh as he finally died.

Adrenaline still coursed fiercely through Jessie's body, and when she heard a soft shuffle off to her left she whirled, bringing her Remington back to the firing position, hammer back and her finger putting tension on the trigger.

A white-faced Alice Sugden was closer to death at that time than at any other in her life. She stood there, holding the horses.

Still shaking, Jessie eased the hammer down and expelled a long breath, trying to rid herself of the remaining tension.

'Are . . . are they all dead?' Alice Sugden asked with a shaky voice.

'Yes, they are.'

'Oh Lord, this is all my fault.'

'Yes, it is.' Jessie's words were harsh but truthful.

'I'm sorry. I panicked. I just wanted to get as far away as possible.'

Jessie let her voice take on a hard edge. 'The next time I tell you to do something, you damn well do it.'

* * *

It was just after noon when Utah Smith noticed the large dust cloud a good distance beyond the town.

He leaned out over the edge of the tower. 'They're comin' in.'

Kinane and Cronkite came out of the commandant's office into the bright sunshine and shielding their eyes, looked up to where the town-tamer was perched.

'Mendoza's back,' he said, pointing out toward the north. 'Looks like he's in a hurry too, the size of the dust cloud he's kickin' up.'

Kinane waved his recognition, and watched as Utah took off his black low-crowned hat and replaced it with a rurale peaked one.

Kinane turned to his friend. 'Are you ready for a fight, old man?'

There was a spark in Cronkite's eyes. 'Let's get it done, kid.'

Kinane smiled and slapped him on the shoulder. 'Don't forget to keep your head down.'

He watched his friend go and then called Hawk over. 'Is everythin' ready?'

'Yeah, Romero's boys are holed up and the townsfolk are off the streets.'

Kinane nodded. 'Well then, let's roll out the welcome mat.'

⋆ ⋆ ⋆

Mendoza was good and mad; and the closer he rode to Las Palomas, the madder he became. He wanted to make someone pay, and the only satisfactory retribution would be for them to die at the hands of the commandant.

His anger clouded his mind so much that when he led his men into the main street of town, it was deserted and he didn't notice. By the time, Mendoza realized something was wrong, it was too late. He'd steered his men blindly into the killing zone.

★　★　★

From his hiding place behind two water barrels in an alley between adjacent adobe buildings, Kinane watched the column ride past. The men who rode the foam-flecked and dust-caked horses were visibly tired. From experience, Kinane knew that once lead started to fly, the bone-weary rurales would snap to it and act like the trained killers they were.

Through the swirling dust the Mexicans left in their wake, Kinane spied Hawk at the window across the street. He used the term *window* loosely because it was more a glassless hole covered by a rag.

The killer signaled that he was ready. Kinane nodded, reaching into his pocket for a pack of Vestas and a foul-tasting thing that passed for a cigarillo. He picked up the first bomb and waited.

★ ★ ★

Cronkite tried to look as inconspicuous as possible, but that was difficult considering that the hat was too big and the jacket too small. He squatted down to show only his head above the wall. The procession was funneled along until it was fed into the plaza. The killing zone.

He waited for a moment as the column drew closer, then he glanced across to Utah Smith. The town-tamer nodded: he was ready to go. Cronkite nodded back, then turned his attention to the Gatling gun. He paused briefly, set his jaw firm, and then started to crank the handle.

The plaza turned into hell on earth. Bullets fizzed through the air in a hail of death. The staccato sound of the two Gatling guns filled the air as they sent their .45–70 caliber payload spewing from rotating muzzles at a steady three hundred and fifty rounds per minute.

Rurales howled with pain while horses screamed almost humanly as they were cut down by an invisible scythe. Bodies were punched out of saddles and Mendoza sawed on his horse's reins, struggling to get it turned.

He yelled wildly at his men to fire their weapons, but they were too busy dying or trying to survive to follow orders. Then a rurale successfully turned his horse and started to flee back the way they'd come. He was quickly followed by another, and then another. Before long a trickle became a surge as more surviving rurales followed suit.

Enraged with what he considered to be cowardice, Mendoza's tirade escalated into a screech, and he drew his sidearm and pointed it at the nearest rurale. Before he could squeeze the trigger, three bullets smashed into his chest from the gun Cronkite was firing.

By this time, the rurales retreating down the main street drew level with Kinane and the others, who unleashed a new kind of hell.

A large fountain of dirt spewed into the air when the first hand-thrown bomb exploded, dispersing its deadly payload. Once more, cries of pain and terror from man and beast filled the air. Horses crumpled, throwing their riders to the ground.

One after another, great geysers of death erupted from the ground, and were swiftly followed by rifle fire from the townsfolk who'd dared to help the Americans.

It finished as abruptly as it began. Some of the rurales escaped, but many were dead, and even more wounded. The result, however, was that Mendoza was deceased and the villagers had their town back. The side of good had sustained not one casualty.

As Kinane wandered through the carnage of downed men and horses, he shook his head at the ghastly and macabre sight. Rurales moaned or cried out in pain, surrounded by chunks of flesh, and bright red blood soaked quickly into the dry earth.

A gunshot from Hawk silenced a thrashing horse and caused Kinane to jump. He turned and frowned at the killer.

'What?'

The gunfighter turned away.

'It's a hell of a business, kid,' Cronkite said as he came up beside his friend.

Kinane shook his head. 'I don't know how we did it, but we did.'

'I guess, seein' as we made this mess, we'd best start cleanin' it up,' the old gunfighter suggested.

Kinane nodded. His friend was right. It was a hell of a business.

13

The four men left Las Palomas the following morning. They rode hard all day and made the river just before nightfall. From there, they would head northeast towards Redemption.

They made camp in the lee of a sandstone cliff, carved out over time by the harsh elements of the desert country. While the others slept, Utah Smith kept watch.

The night was cool and relatively quiet. Clouds scudded across the desert sky which caused the pale moonlight to flicker and die on occasion.

A muffled disturbance near the horses drew the town-tamer's attention and put him on edge. It wasn't much, just a snort followed by the stomp of hooves.

Utah drew his six-gun and skirted cautiously around the camp, coming up on the blind side of where the horses were picketed. It was then that he noticed the shadow moving between the mounts.

Utah thumbed back the gun hammer. 'Hold it right there, hombre, or you're a dead man.'

'Son of a bitch, Utah, you scared the hell out of me.'

'Hawk?' the town-tamer queried. 'What are you doin' out here?'

'Thought I heard a noise so I came out to look,' the killer answered.

Utah thought about it for a moment and eased his gun back into its holster. 'Did you see anythin'?'

Hawk moved closer to the town-tamer. 'No, must have been a coyote.'

Utah turned instinctively and looked out across the darkened desert. 'Yeah, might well have been,' he agreed.

Something dawned on him. He'd not heard a coyote all night. When they were about, you couldn't miss them. He turned back to voice his opinion to Hawk, but never even got halfway.

The knife in Hawk's fist drove between the town-tamer's ribs and pierced his heart. At the same time, a calloused hand clamped firmly over Utah's mouth, and stifled any noise that might escape from his lips.

The man stiffened briefly, then his body went limp. Hawk lowered him gently to the ground so not to make a noise. He withdrew the knife, and the coppery smell of fresh blood reached his nostrils. Hawk wiped the blade on Utah's jacket and slipped it back into his boot. He quietly eased his already saddled horse away from the picket line and out into the desert. He still had a lot of riding to do if he wanted to catch up with the women.

* * *

Kinane and Cronkite stared down at the cold, stiff body of Utah Smith. A large patch of desert sand beside his body had turned a deep red from the blood that had been expelled from him.

'Now, why would Hawk go and do somethin' like that?' Cronkite wondered aloud. 'It just don't make no sense.'

Kinane remained silent, and pondered the answer himself. Utah was to have awoken him around two for his turn at watch, but it hadn't eventuated. This was the reason. It had gone unnoticed because the other two men were tired. Just plain wore out, as Cronkite had put it.

When the sun rose that morning, the body of the dead town-tamer was what they'd found.

'Nope,' Cronkite said again, 'I don't get it. What does he have to gain by slippin' away in the middle of the night and killin' Smith along the way?'

'The girl,' Kinane declared. 'He's gone after Alice Sugden.'

'But why?' asked the old gunfighter. 'He's gettin' five thousand dollars the same as us.'

'He wants all the money for himself,' Kinane explained. 'Why have just five thousand when you can have it all?

Thirty thousand dollars.'

'Son of a bitch,' Cronkite cursed.

'Exactly. We need to go. Now!'

* ★ *

'I said to drop your gun,' Hawk hissed at Jessie. 'I won't tell you again.'

The secret service agent stood firm, her hand resting on her gun butt. 'I can't do that, Hawk.'

The killer looked at her incredulously. 'What? You're willin' to die for her?' He pointed at Alice as she took refuge behind Jessie.

Hawk had pushed his horse near to death in his efforts to catch them. Now he was determined that he would not be stopped. There was far too much money at stake. It was late in the afternoon, and the three of them were maybe a day from Redemption, where they were to meet up with Bell.

Jessie and Alice had been resting their horses in a stand of cottonwoods beside a lazy, slow-flowing creek when

Hawk had caught up with them. Not one known for his patience, he'd come right out with his intentions, and was at this moment in the middle of a one-sided negotiation that was quickly going south.

'Not going to happen Hawk,' Jessie said stubbornly.

'Well, then — ' The killer smiled coldly. ' — you'd best get that there little filly to step to one side so we can get this over and done with.'

'Jessie?' Alice whimpered.

'Do as he says, Alice,' Jessie cautioned. 'Move out of the way.'

Alice Sugden hesitantly moved to one side.

Hawk's smile never wavered as he slid his Colt back into its holster. 'Any time you're ready.'

There was a moment of uncertainty as Jessie stood like a statue and tried to settle her nerves. She stared into the killer's cold, smiling eyes, and a wave of calm finally came over her. Then she did something that unnerved Hawk.

She smiled at him — a broad smile that showed her even teeth — then she went for her gun.

Her smooth draw was unbelievably fast and it took Hawk by surprise. Even as she squeezed the trigger, the killer's gun was roaring in defiance and the slug caught Jessie high in the chest, knocking her flat on her back.

Hawk felt the searing burn as the bullet from Jessie's Remington scored out flesh along his ribs. He grunted in a mixture of surprise and pain, but kept his feet. He lurched forward and stood over the prone form of the secret service agent. A bright red stain spread across the front of her shirt.

He spat on the ground. 'I'll give you one thing, missy, you sure had some guts. A lot more than I gave you credit for.'

Hawk turned to Alice Sugden. She cowered away from his gaze and let tears roll down her face unimpeded. 'As for you, get up on that horse of yours. You're about to make me rich.'

172

Kinane and Cronkite found Jessie just before dark. She lay propped against a deadfall where she'd managed to drag herself, barely conscious and still bleeding from the chest wound.

They both knelt beside her, and while Cronkite peeled open her shirt to check out the wound, Kinane asked her what had happened.

'That son of a bitch turned up, and was set on . . . set on . . . ' She coughed, and her chest rattled from the slow fluid build-up. 'He was set on taking . . . taking Alice.'

Jessie took another deep, gurgling breath. 'I couldn't let . . . let him take her without a . . . a fight. Bastard was too . . . too quick.'

Kinane patted her arm. 'Take it easy. We'll get him.' The gunfighter looked questioningly over at his friend.

Cronkite shook his head, and Kinane felt something he'd not felt in a long time: loss. He'd known that Jessie had

173

made an impression on his hardened exterior; but until now, watching her dying before his own eyes, he hadn't realized how much.

Jessie broke the gloomy silence. 'It's okay. I know . . . I'm dying. I can . . . I can feel it.'

She coughed, and a small trickle of blood spilled over her lips. Kinane wiped it away with his thumb.

'I'm sorry, Jessie, if I'd just . . . '

He felt her hand on his arm. 'It's okay, not . . . not your fault. Do one thing for . . . for me?'

'Sure,' he said, a lump in his throat.

Jessie spoke, but her voice was no more than a whisper, so Kinane leaned in close and put his ear next to her lips.

'Let . . . let them go,' she said weakly. 'Your wife and . . . and daughter. Be the man that they . . . they loved.'

And then she was gone.

Kinane stared at her still, almost childlike form for a few moments, and then shifted his gaze to Cronkite.

'I'm sorry, kid,' he said sadly, 'but at

least she ain't hurtin' no more.'

They buried Jessie under a large cottonwood where the creek passed slowly by.

The following morning, when they rode out for Redemption, hanging from a cross crudely fashioned from cotton-wood branches was the chain and crucifix that Kinane had carried in his pocket.

*   *   *

Redemption was a frontier town which had begun as a hell-on-earth place where outlaws took refuge when they were one jump ahead of a posse. With no law of any kind, it had been ideal for fugitive border-jumpers until ten years previously, when the Texas Rangers had sent a troop to clean it up.

It had taken a considerable amount of time, but what had been a haven for the wanted fugitive had now evolved into an upstanding community. A town of two hundred questionable souls had exploded, and the population had climbed to nine hundred law-abiding citizens. Now there was only one problem. The name: Redemption. That was about to change, and within the coming weeks the now-bustling town was scheduled to vote on another name and the bad old days would be left in the past. The two choices were New Haven or Prosperity, and now the forerunner appeared to be the latter.

One other thing that had changed with the introduction of law and order was the names of town businesses. Grange's Emporium had once been the Redemption Emporium; The Three Dogs saloon was now The Gold Coin, and Helga's Hen House had changed its name to Helen's Men's Retreat. Subtle changes which, coupled with many new buildings and establishments, changed the overall look of the town. In the old Outlaw's Rest hotel, known now as the Traveler's Rest, Hawk faced Bell and laid down what he wanted from the government man.

The room, at four dollars a night, reflected the changing times in the town. It was large and spacious, fully carpeted, and dark timber paneling covered the bottom half of the walls while the top half was wallpapered. A small chandelier hung from the central part of the ceiling, and numerous paintings were spaced evenly about the room. The bed was a large iron-framed affair with a coil-spring mattress, topped with clean linen and fine blankets. The timber furniture was hand-crafted and polished to a high sheen.

'I want all the reward money, or I ride away and you never see the girl again,' Hawk snapped.

Bell was still reeling from the information that the senator and his wife were dead, along with three of the rescue party, including Jessie.

'She was fast, alright,' her murderer had gloated, 'but not fast enough. She had more guts than I gave her credit for. You taught her well.'

Bell said nothing.

'Well, what about it?' Hawk asked now, impatiently.

Bell gave the killer a harsh look. 'I'm going to see you hang, you murderous bastard.'

'Yeah, yeah. The money?'

'I'll have to get it from the bank. It may take a little time.'

'You've got until three tomorrow afternoon,' Hawk stated. 'There's some warehouses on the outskirts of town that folks use to store stuff in. You'll find me there. Make sure you have the money, or like I said, you'll never see the girl alive again. Oh, and no law.'

'How do I know that the girl is still alive?' Bell asked.

'You don't,' the killer said. 'You'll just have to wait and see.'

The secret service agent trembled with anger as he watched Hawk leave the room. He cursed softly under his breath, and walked over to the brandy decanter and glasses that sat on a polished table in a corner. He turned a glass up the right way and filled it, then tossed the liquor down in one gulp and stared at the empty vessel. The next thing he knew was the smashing sound as it shattered after he'd thrown it at the far wall.

He decided there and then that he would do whatever it took to kill that man.

* * *

Kinane and Cronkite rode into Redemption late in the afternoon on bone-weary horses that would have been lucky to last another mile. They left them at the livery and set about finding Bell before they tended to themselves.

They found him in another of the re-named saloons, this one called the Double Deuce. As luck would have it, the first establishment they had checked was the Traveler's Rest, and the clerk had told the two grime-covered men where Bell was.

Kinane and Cronkite walked in through the saloon's double doors, still brushing trail dust from their clothes. They stopped and looked around the well-lit room, but the pair couldn't see Bell for the crowd. The place was jam-packed with customers, and the noise was somewhere between loud and a dull roar.

Cronkite followed his friend as he shouldered his way through the crowd and up to the bar, where he squeezed between two cowhands and worked at getting the attention of one of the three bartenders. After a couple of minutes trying, he finally managed to alert the smallest of the men behind the bar, who was as bald as a billiard ball.

'What can I get you, mister?' He almost shouted to be heard over the noise.

'I'm lookin' for a feller. I was told he was here. He'd be got up in a suit of clothes like they dress back East. He would have been in town for a while.'

The barkeep gave the matter minimal thought before he said, 'Over in the far corner. Front left. You'll find him there.'

Kinane nodded. 'Obliged.'

Cronkite followed him to where Bell sat at a polished but scarred round hardwood table, hunched forward over a half-full shot glass. Beside it was a two-thirds-empty bottle of rye. They stopped in front of the table and waited for Bell to raise his eyes.

When he did, they were red and glassy. He was well on his way to being smashed. Through the haze of drunkenness, the secret service man recognized them both. His eyes widened and instantly filled with rage. He fumbled for his gun, tucked away out of sight in its shoulder holster.

Kinane leaned forward and clamped an iron grip on Bell's arm, holding it immobile.

'Let me go, damn you,' he spluttered, voice starting to slur. 'I'm going to kill you. You were supposed to keep her alive. And now look at what happened.'

'Take it easy, Bell.' Kinane spoke just loud enough for him to hear.

The gunfighter used his other hand

to retrieve the man's pistol. Kinane dropped it on the table, then he and Cronkite sat down.

'I take it you've seen Hawk?'

'That damn murdering son of a bitch,' Bell spat. 'After I get the girl back, I'm going to kill him too.'

The last few words came out as a snarl as he lunged for the six-gun on the table. His hand almost made it, but Cronkite's fist crashed solidly into his jaw and stopped him cold. The mix of the blow and the alcohol did their work: Bell's glassy eyes closed and he was out like a light, face-down on the table top.

'Come on, kid,' the old gunfighter said. 'Let's get him back to his room. Come mornin' he'll be sober enough to talk some sense into.'

Kinane nodded. 'Yeah, let's go.'

They managed to lift Bell from his seat, and between them half-dragged and half carried him out of the Double Deuce. Nobody seemed to notice.

14

Bell moaned, held a trembling hand against his throbbing head, and slowly opened his eyes. He closed them tight as bright sunlight lanced through them, causing his head more pain.

'About time you came alive,' said a gruff voice.

Bell's eyes snapped open and his head swung to look in the direction of the voice. He stared at Cronkite through a fog of misery, trying to decide what his next move would be.

'Do I have to hit you again?' the old gunfighter asked.

Bell let out a sigh and relaxed. 'No. That was you?'

'Yeah,' Cronkite said, 'it seemed better to do it that way than to shoot you.'

'Appreciate it,' Bell whispered hoarsely. 'Where's Kinane?'

'I'm here,' Kinane answered as he

pulled himself out of an ornately hand-tooled lounge chair.

Bell sat up and swung his legs over the side of the bed. Apart from jacket and shoes, he was still clad in the clothes he'd worn the previous day. He waited for his head to stop spinning before he let his gaze settle on Kinane.

'I must apologise for my behavior,' he said. 'It was unforgivable.'

'It was understandable,' the gunfighter allowed. 'As a matter of fact, I feel the same way. But we can't undo what's been done. All that we can do is get the girl back in one piece.'

'What about Hawk?' Bell snapped.

'He'll get what's comin' to him,' the gunfighter promised. 'Make no mistake.'

'What does he want?' Cronkite asked.

'He wants all of the money, or he's goin' to kill the girl.'

'When does he want it?' Kinane asked.

'Today,' Bell explained. 'He's given me until three o'clock this afternoon.'

'I take it you have the money?' Cronkite asked.

'It's in the bank,' he told them. 'I can get it before I have to meet him. Apparently, there are some warehouses on the outskirts of town. He said to take the money there. And, of course, no law.'

'Well, you won't have any law,' Kinane informed him. 'But you will have us.'

'I don't know,' Bell protested. 'I don't want to get Alice killed because I turn up with you two. I've already got Jessie weighing on my conscience, I'd not care to have the Sugden girl too.'

'He won't kill the girl,' Kinane assured him, 'as long as the money is there and he thinks he's goin' to get it, Hawk won't do anythin' to put that in jeopardy.'

Bell thought for a moment, then said, 'Okay, we'll do it that way. But if you're wrong . . . '

'I won't be.'

'Well, I guess it's settled then,'

Cronkite put in. 'Now, who wants somethin' to eat? I'm starvin'.'

Bell started at the mention of food. Cronkite smiled wickedly as the secret service man turned green.

* * *

There were five warehouses in all. Five large buildings that looked more like oversized barns than anything else. Each had large double-doors, spacious lofts and a gabled roof. They were situated centrally, in a u-shape around an open area that allowed wagons to turn around and unload without any problems.

Behind one of the warehouses was a corral used to hold the animals of the teamsters who freighted in all the town's produce. Scattered about behind the other storage houses were large oak trees that had stood there long before the town itself.

The three men stood at the open double doors of the southernmost warehouse. There were two more on the east side of the cul-de-sac, and another couple directly to the north of where they stood.

'What do you think?' Cronkite asked Kinane.

Kinane didn't answer straight away, choosing instead to keep running his eyes over what was out there as he assessed the situation. One by one, he let his gaze linger on the buildings, and searched for things out of place. As he was about to answer his friend, he saw a flicker of movement up in an opening of the loft on the east side.

'Cronk, did you see it?' he asked, lips hardly moving.

'Yeah, kid, I got it.' He slipped away and left Kinane standing there with Bell.

'What's going on, Kinane?' Bell asked the gunfighter.

'Up in the loft of the building to our right,' Kinane explained, 'there was some movement at the hatch where they winch goods in. I saw the barrel of a rifle.'

'I can't see anything.'

'They're there.'

'Well, well,' interrupted a voice from the doorway of the warehouse directly across the cul-de-sac from where they stood, 'look who's back from Mexico.'

Kinane judged that there was maybe thirty yards between him and Hawk. Every fiber of his being wanted to draw his Peacemaker and shoot the killer where he stood, but two things stopped him. One was the distance. At this range, he was unsure whether he could kill him with the first shot. The second was the girl, Alice Sugden. Hawk had a man up in the loft, but he couldn't be sure that there wasn't one with her as well.

'Where is the girl, Hawk?' Bell called out.

'She's here,' the killer confirmed.

'Bring her out.'

'Nope,' Hawk shouted, shaking his head. 'You come on over here and you can see for yourself. And don't forget the money.' He pointed at the valise that was on the ground next to the secret service man. Bell picked it up, and he and Kinane stepped forward.

'Not you, Kinane,' Hawk called out. 'You stay right there.'

'I'll be fine,' Bell assured him.

'Walk slow,' the gunfighter instructed him.

Kinane watched as Bell slowly marched across the empty yard toward the smiling killer. When he reached the building across the way, both men disappeared inside.

Kinane lifted his gaze, directed it towards the loft where the suspected shooter was concealed, and wondered how Cronkite had fared in his attempt to deal with the bushwhacker.

His thoughts were interrupted by a gunshot.

'Ah hell,' Kinane cursed as he drew his Peacemaker and ran towards the warehouse that Hawk and Bell were in.

★ ★ ★

Cronkite had moved fleetingly around the back of the east side warehouse and slipped in through a side door. Immediately he ducked behind a stack of hundred-pound flour barrels and waited. When nothing happened, he eased out and looked around, seeing only stacked crates of merchandise and more barrels of produce.

In the middle of the central aisle was a large freight wagon. It was stacked high with goods and had a stained grey-white tarp pulled over the load and tied down.

Behind the wagon, the old gunfighter spotted a set of solid timber stairs that led up into the loft. Without thinking twice, Cronkite thumbed back the hammer on his six-gun, and swiftly and as quietly as possible moved to the base of the stairs.

Cronkite stopped briefly at the foot of them before he began to climb slowly, one foot after the other. As luck would have it, the stairs themselves were finely constructed, and none of them made any noise as he placed a foot down to take his weight.

As his head approached the opening at the top, Cronkite heard the single gunshot.

Without hesitation, he took the rest of the steps two at a time and moved over the crest at the top of the stairs and into the loft. Cronkite saw the bushwhacker at the open hatch, his rifle to his shoulder as he sighted down the barrel. The old gunfighter raised his Colt and took aim at the man's broad back.

As he started to squeeze the trigger, the bushwhacker's rifle whiplashed. The man grunted as the .45 caliber slug from Cronkite's Colt slammed into his back. He staggered forward on wobbly legs, pitched headlong through the opening, and thudded onto the hard-packed ground below.

Cronkite hurried forward to look out the hatch and saw Kinane below, gun drawn and looking up in his direction. Cronkite gave him a salute and waved him on before turning on his heel and rushing back to the stairs.

When Kinane entered the warehouse, he found Alice Sugden tied up on the floor and Bell a short distance from her, in a prone position with a gunshot wound in the upper left of his chest. Beside him was a small nickel-plated Derringer.

'What the hell did you do?' Kinane asked him as he ripped open the wounded man's shirt to examine the bullet hole.

'I thought I could get him . . . for Jessie,' Bell gasped out. 'But I guess he expected I'd do something stupid. He was waiting for it.'

Cronkite came running into the warehouse. 'What happened? What was the gunshot?'

'Bell here tried to play hero and got shot for his troubles,' Kinane explained. 'Untie the girl Cronk.'

Cronkite moved to Alice and worked on her bonds.

'Where did he go, Bell?' Kinane asked him.

Bell shook his head. 'I don't know.'

'I heard a horse out the back,' Alice put in. 'After he shot the man, he scooped up the bag and ran off that way.'

The gunfighter climbed to his feet. 'Look after 'em, Cronk. I'm goin' after Hawk.'

'But he's on a damn horse,' Cronkite called after him.

When Kinane exited the back doors of the warehouse he found what he'd expected. Another horse, a bay, was tied to one of the corral posts. Two riders, two horses.

The gunfighter ran across to the horse and leapt into the saddle. He leaned forward, wrenched the reins loose from the post, and swung his mount about.

Tell-tale dust signs indicated that Hawk was riding hard on the main trail that headed east away from Redemption. Kinane spurred the mount forward, and it didn't take long before the horse was running hard.

He followed the dust trail created by the leading horse, riding hands and heels, urging his mount to go faster. It responded, and the gap was closing. The trail stretched out before Kinane in a straight line for a mile before it climbed up the first of a series of boulder- and tree-strewn ridges.

When they reached the foot of the climb, the horse was still going strong, and it took the winding climb with ease. As the trail topped out, Kinane drew up and saw that Hawk's horse had slowed dramatically.

A surge of hope flooded through the gunfighter, and he set the horse downslope after the killer. It was soon evident as to why Hawk's mount had slowed. The trail was filled with ruts and corrugations from constant weather and use. He guessed that the horse in front had injured a hoof in one.

When he hit the bottom of the slope, Kinane had gained a lot more ground. Then he saw Hawk turn his horse off the trail and ride toward a large formation of granite boulders. The gunfighter cut off to follow the killer.

Hawk leapt from his lame horse,

dived behind a clump of rocks, and waited for Kinane to get close enough before he opened fire.

The gunfighter saw the puffs of blue-grey gunsmoke and felt his mount shudder beneath him as a bullet found its mark. The animal started to go down on its nose as its front legs started to buckle. Kinane kicked free of the stirrups and hit the ground running. He fired two wild shots to keep Hawk's head down while he found some cover.

He dived behind a rock as Hawk opened fire once more. Stone chips flew from the rock and sliced through the air like miniature razors. Ricochets screamed off into the distance.

Kinane rose and fired three shots which caused Hawk to duck back behind cover. The gunfighter dropped down and replaced the empty cartridges in the Peacemaker. He looked about to assess his position. Now he was at a disadvantage due to Hawk holding the high ground. Judging from the direction of the last shots, he was aiming to get higher.

Kinane's only option was to circle right through the rocks and brush; left would bring him out into the open. He eased up and looked over the rock he was sheltering behind. Immediately, Hawk fired again, and more stone chips flew: a sliver nicked Kinane's cheek and drew a small drop of blood.

The shot had given away Hawk's position for the moment. Kinane fired two shots in the killer's direction and, bent low, started to quickly move to the right.

Hawk saw Kinane move and fired at him while he was on the run. Small eruptions of dirt rose at the gunfighter's heel as the bullets ploughed into the earth. More cracked through the brush as Kinane sheltered behind it. Somehow, he had to get above Hawk.

The gunfighter saw that there was a rock shelf behind Hawk's sheltered position, and guessed that it was probably his destination. From there, he would certainly have a superior field of fire. The only thing to do was to reach it before Hawk could.

Kinane worked his way between two large boulders and started the climb towards his goal. It was made easier because Hawk had stopped firing, which told him that the killer was on the move as well.

The gunfighter threw caution to the wind and ascended towards the ledge as fast as he could. Still no gunfire came.

When he reached the ledge, Kinane was blowing hard, and tried to catch his breath. He looked about for Hawk, and saw him as he appeared at the far end of the flat rock formation.

The killer looked surprised to see him and brought his gun up to fire. For some inexplicable reason neither man shot. They stood with guns aimed at each another as they sucked in great gulps of air.

'Seems we have us a bit of a standoff,' Hawk said hoarsely, still puffing.

'It would seem that way,' Kinane agreed.

'The way I see it,' Hawk observed, 'this can go down one of two ways. We can take our chances and both pull the trigger and maybe one of us will live.'

'Or?'

'Or we can settle it the old-fashioned way. Put up our guns and may the fastest man win.'

Kinane thought about it for a moment and looked at the distance between them. It was twenty feet at the most. He thought about Jessie, and his anger built. A dark rage threatened to consume him as he stared at her killer. He also remembered the promise he'd made to her as he'd stood over her grave under the large cottonwood tree.

His anger abated and a calmness came over him, and he began to relax.

'Sure, let's do it,' Kinane said with a coolness that was designed to get under Hawk's skin. 'You put your gun up first.'

'Yeah, right,' the killer snorted derisively. 'Then you'll shoot me down where I stand. How dumb do you think I am?'

'I've never shot down an unarmed man, Hawk. As for you, I don't reckon you could say the same. You may not trust me, but I sure as hell don't trust you. Your choice.'

Hawk thought about it for a time and Kinane could see his uncertainty as he fought an inner war. After a little more time, he dropped his Colt into its holster. 'Alright, your turn.'

Kinane holstered his Peacemaker and the outlaw smiled.

'So, I guess this is where we find out, huh?' Hawk observed.

'Find out what?'

'Why, who's fastest of course.' The killer radiated confidence as he prepared for what was about to happen.

Kinane shook his head. 'No, this is where you die.'

Hawk's face dropped, and for a fleeting moment there was uncertainty in him about the outcome. He pushed it to one side and smiled again. 'Whenever you're ready.'

Kinane never blinked. 'Call it.'

There was a period of silence, a pregnant pause which was only disturbed by the buzz of a fly whose sound was almost deafening in the quiet.

Hawk's eye flickered and his right hand dropped to his Colt. His draw was smooth and in the blink of an eye the gun was level and his index finger was taking up what little slack was in the trigger.

Thunder rolled along the rock shelf and a wisp of gun-smoke drifted up from Kinane's Peacemaker. The .45 caliber slug hammered into Hawk's chest, driving him up onto his toes. A look of disbelief spread across his face as he couldn't believe he'd been outdrawn.

He staggered back and tried to regain his balance, stopped at the edge of the shelf, and gave Kinane a pained smile. Kinane lifted the Peacemaker and shot the killer through his forehead. That last bullet sent Hawk over the edge. Kinane stood quietly and stared off into the distance, devoid of feeling.

Four days after the death of Hawk, three men stood outside the Redemption livery saying their good-byes.

'Will you be alright to find it?' Kinane asked Bell.

The secret service man nodded. 'I think so.'

'How's the wound?' Cronkite asked him.

'It's okay. The doctor said just to take it easy and it should be fine. I was just lucky the bullet didn't hit nothing vital. I'll take my time, say good-bye, and then ride back here. Lay up for a few more days and then head back to Washington.'

'What about Alice?' Kinane asked.

'She's doing as well as can be expected,' Bell told them. 'She'll stay here, then go back to Washington with me. What about you two? Where are you headed?'

'I'm headed to Kansas,' Kinane explained. 'I'm goin' home.'

'And I'm goin' with him,' Cronkite supplied. 'My days of gun work are done. I only took this job to get it out of my system. Now I have.'

Bell nodded and climbed onto the rented buckskin horse, 'Good luck then, gentlemen. I hope it all works out for you. Although I still can't understand why neither of you accepted any payment.'

They shook hands and watched Bell go before Cronkite said, 'Are you ready to go home, kid?'

Kinane stared off to the south. He let his mind wander briefly and could see the cottonwood tree with the grave beneath it. He blinked once and it was gone.

'Yeah, Cronk,' he said softly. 'I'm ready to go home.'

We do hope that you have enjoyed reading this large print book.

Did you know that all of our titles are available for purchase?

We publish a wide range of high quality large print books including:
Romances, Mysteries, Classics
General Fiction
Non Fiction and Westerns

Special interest titles available in large print are:
The Little Oxford Dictionary
Music Book, Song Book
Hymn Book, Service Book

Also available from us courtesy of Oxford University Press:
Young Readers' Dictionary
(large print edition)
Young Readers' Thesaurus
(large print edition)

For further information or a free brochure, please contact us at:
Ulverscroft Large Print Books Ltd.,
The Green, Bradgate Road, Anstey,
Leicester, LE7 7FU, England.
Tel: (00 44) **0116 236 4325**
Fax: (00 44) **0116 234 0205**

THE VALERON CODE

Terrell L. Bowers

When Rodney Mason is hired by a banker to help his sister, it seems like just another job. But he finds more than he bargained for in Deliverance, Colorado. The opposition is ruthless, and the victim someone who can change his world. When an ambush leaves Rod vulnerable and unable to fight back, word is sent to his brothers and cousins. Within hours, Wyatt and Jared Valeron are dispatched to aid their kin. The odds against them mount, but a Valeron doesn't know how to quit . . .

THE BLOODY TRAIL TO REDEMPTION

Paxton Johns

English aristocrat Born Gallant is riding to Dodge City when he is attacked and left to die. Initially relieved when rescued by a lawman and his posse, they then accuse him of murder. A witness has sworn that he saw Gallant stab a Kansas senator, and it seems certain he will hang for a crime he did not commit. With the help of some old friends, Gallant uncovers a web of political intrigue and vengeance — but will he be able to unmask the true murderer?

RIMROCK RENEGADE

Ned Oaks

Released after spending five years in prison for a crime he didn't commit, Hank Chesham only wants to return home to his ranch, the Rimrock, and resume his old life. But then he discovers that he has been betrayed by both his wife, Phoebe, and his best friend, Ted Flynn, who have conspired to steal the Rimrock from him. Now Chesham has but one thing on his mind: vengeance. But before he can take action, Flynn unleashes his hired killers . . .

THE LAST GUN

Peter Wilson

Jack Crawford, badly wounded in the final action of the Civil War, returns home to discover that his parents have been massacred, and the family ranch has fallen into the hands of empire-building newcomer Vic Bannon. When Crawford becomes town sheriff, he finds himself in opposition to the ruthless Bannon, with his own brother Clay helping to force the homesteaders and farmers out of the valley. As the threat of range war looms, Crawford must defend the home he now barely recognizes, before it disappears forever.

FLAME AND THUNDER

Ben Bridges

It stands to be the biggest oil well in the territory, provided wildcatter Bud Bishop can bring it in before his lease runs out. But Hugh Quillan wants to move in and keep the spoils for himself. So Bishop's backers hire freelance fighting man Carter O'Brien to keep Quillan's bullyboys in check. But the closer it comes to the deadline, the harder Quillan starts to play. With the threat of a full-scale war looming, O'Brien does the only thing he can — he makes sure his guns are loaded . . .